MARGARET K. McELDERRY BOOKS
New York London Toronto Sydney New Delhi

* MARGARET K. McELDERRY BOOKS * An imprint of Simon & Schuster Children's Publishing Division * 1230 Avenue of the Americas, New York, New York 10020 *
This book is a work of fiction. Any references to historical events, real people, or real places are used fictitiously. Other names, characters, places, and events are products of the author's imagination, and any resemblance to actual events or places or persons, living or dead, is entirely coincidental.
* Text copyright © 2014 by William Alexander * Cover illustration copyright © 2015 by Stéphanie Hans * All rights reserved, including the right of reproduction in whole or in part in any form. * MARGARET K. McELDERRY BOOKS is a trademark of Simon & Schuster, Inc. * For information about special discounts for bulk purchases, please contact Simon & Schuster Special Sales at 1-866-506-1949 or business@simonandschuster.com. * The Simon & Schuster Speakers Bureau can bring authors to your live event. For more information or to book an event, contact the Simon & Schuster Speakers Bureau at 1-866-248-3049 or visit our website at www.simonspeakers.com. * Also available in a Margaret K. McElderry Books hardcover edition * The text for this book is set in Adobe Caslon Pro. * Manufactured in the United States of America * 0815 OFF * First Margaret K. McElderry Books paperback edition September 2015 * 10 9 8 7 6 5 4 3 2 1 * The Library of Congress has cataloged the hardcover edition as follows: * Alexander, William (William Joseph), 1976– * Ambassador / William Alexander.—First edition. * p. cm. * Summary: Appointed Earth's ambassador to the universe, eleven-year-old Gabe Fuentes faces two sets of "alien" problems when he discovers his parents are illegal aliens and face deportation, and the Earth is in the path of a destructive alien force causing multiple mass extinctions. * ISBN 978-1-4424-9764-1 (hc) * ISBN 978-1-4424-9765-8 (pbk) * ISBN 978-1-4424-9766-5 (eBook) * [1. Science fiction. 2. Human-alien encounters—Fiction. 3. Illegal aliens—Fiction. 4. Mexican Americans—Fiction. 5. Ambassadors—Fiction.] I. Title. * PZ7.A3787Am 2014 * [Fic]—dc23 * 2013037333

Para mis sobrinos Isaac y Navarro

PART ONE
SELECTED

1

The Envoy tossed itself at the world.

An ambassador's business had left it stranded on the moon for years and decades. During all that time it tried to patch together a return capsule from Soviet equipment abandoned on the surface. But this had never actually worked, and now it needed to hurry, so it gave up on the capsule and built a cannon instead. Then the Envoy aimed itself and its cannon at the world.

This was not the tricky part.

Moving through vacuum for several days was not the tricky part either. The Envoy had no ship, no craft, no transportation. It had only itself: the spherical, purple transparency of its own substance. It clenched its outer layers, becoming glass-like to bounce radiation away and keep itself from dehydrating. But it remained clear enough to let light in. All of it was sensitive to light. It was its own big, purple eyeball. The Envoy watched the approaching planet with all of itself, and enjoyed the view.

The nightside of the globe grew large ahead. Constellations of bright and artificial light stretched out across landmasses. The Envoy expected to land in Russia again, or possibly in China, but North America stretched out below it.

The first hints of atmosphere scraped against its skin. The Envoy winced. This was going to hurt. *This* would be the tricky part.

The Envoy became a blind eye, opaque, closing itself and all its senses. The view was about to become too searingly bright to appreciate. Air turned to plasma against the friction of the Envoy's passage.

It shed several layers of scorched self. Then it slowed down by expanding, thinning its substance against air currents like the stretched skin of a flying squirrel or a flying fish or a flying squid. It became its own parachute— though it didn't slow down nearly as much as a real parachute would have. The Envoy tumbled into a rough glide. It became transparent again, letting light pass through it, trying to see where it was going and what it was falling toward. It failed to see very much.

The Envoy smacked into a small pond in an urban

park. The noise and splash startled several geese, ducks, catfish, and turtles.

It sank into the mud and muck at the very bottom and felt itself gradually cool, losing the sting of impact. It needed time to collect itself—though not literally, for which it was grateful. Its substance remained in one single piece.

A few curious fish tried to nibble the Envoy. It tried to ignore them. Then it made a limb and shoed them away. Finally it stretched out and relearned how to swim. It had been a long time since the Envoy had lived in an aquatic environment, but now it remembered how to wave and ripple like a manta ray. It swam up to the surface of the pond. There it carefully observed the shore, the surrounding park, and the playgrounds.

The Envoy spent many days floating and recovering from planetfall before it noticed Gabriel Sandro Fuentes.

2

Gabe sat on a swing and watched his toddler siblings, Andrés and Noemi.

Noemi sat underneath a plastic slide and poured handfuls of sand over her sandals. Andrés, her twin brother, climbed up and down the stairs that led to the slide. He didn't actually like the slide itself, but he loved going up and down the stairs. They both seemed focused and content with what they were doing.

Gabe kept a close eye on them anyway.

The chains of his swing creaked like door hinges as he swayed back and forth. His friend Frankie sat in the other swing and complained. Gabe was dark and shorter than his average peer, while Frankie was pale, tall, and spindly thin.

"Why do you have to babysit today?" Frankie asked.

"It's Thursday," Gabe answered, as though that explained everything.

"So?" said Frankie.

"So Mom tutors on Thursdays. I can't remember what subject she's got today. Might be Spanish. Might be math. I hope it isn't standardized test prep. She *hates* test prep. And my sister has a restaurant shift, and then Dad has his own shift later. He's making dinner now. So that leaves me to watch the twins."

"Huh," said Frankie—the uncomprehending grunt of an only child who has never had to watch anyone else. "I wish I could come over for dinner. I'd rather have your dad's cooking than eat with my mom while she glares at me."

"You can't, though," said Gabe. "We're *supposed* to be avoiding each other right now."

"Yeah," Frankie said sadly.

The other kids playing nearby were either very much younger or very much older than Gabe and Frankie. Two older boys played basketball in a court adjacent to the playground. They shouted and cursed each other out. It sounded angry. It sounded vicious. Gabe glanced their way whenever an especially sharp curse cut the air. But it didn't look like they were fighting. Not really. So it was probably just aggressive conversation. The cursing might have been part of their game.

Gabe looked back at the twins. Noemi still sat under

the slide with her handfuls of sand. Andrés kept climbing the stairs.

"My mom is pretty mad," said Frankie. "Have you noticed how she seems to get taller whenever she gets mad?"

Gabe nodded without looking away from the twins. He had noticed. Frankie's mom turned into a towering statue of wrathful ice whenever she got mad.

"She's sending me to live with my dad for the rest of the summer," Frankie went on. "In California."

That got Gabe's attention. "Really?"

"Really," said Frankie. "She puts me on a plane tonight."

"Tonight?" This was a terrible thing. Frankie was Gabe's only friend within walking distance. They usually spent whole summers together—except for the summers Frankie spent with his dad. And this summer wasn't supposed to be one of those. "So we don't have time to talk her out of it?" He tried to think of apologies and promises that might somehow appease Frankie's mom.

"Don't try to talk her out of it," said Frankie. "Really. Don't. It won't work. And at least in California I won't have to see her glare at me for a while." He kicked the sand under his swing with one foot. "I think we got the fuel mix wrong."

"I think we shouldn't have used a metal pipe," Gabe told him. "Model rockets are usually paper and plastic.

Lightweight. They cause less damage when they hit things. And they're less likely to just fall over, spin in place, and spew flames."

"But the pipe looked like it *wanted* to be a rocket, just sitting there in the garage," Frankie said. "It was all shiny. Like it *dreamed* of becoming a rocket rather than a piece of plumbing. Anyway, thanks for saying it was your idea."

"You're welcome," said Gabe.

"It kind of *was* your idea," said Frankie.

"No, it wasn't," said Gabe. "Did any of the lawn furniture survive?"

"None of it," said Frankie, his voice morose.

"Is lawn furniture expensive?" Gabe asked, a bit worried.

"Probably," said Frankie. "I think she plans to take it out of us in leaf-raking and snow-shoveling later. But right now she doesn't want to see either of us, so she's banishing me to California. She'll probably just ignore you if she sees you around. Were your parents mad?"

"Sort of," said Gabe. "Dad tried to be, but he kept laughing. Mom was angrier, but mostly she was just relieved we didn't die."

He watched Noemi sift sand. Then he looked for Andrés and noticed that Andrés was no longer climbing stairs.

Gabe couldn't see him. He scanned the various small

children, looking for a familiar one. He stood up from his swing, still searching, ready to run but not yet sure which direction to run in.

Noemi still sat under the slide.

Andrés didn't seem to be anywhere.

Then Gabe found him, finally. The toddler had left the playground, stepped onto the grass, and approached a very old woman sitting on a park bench. The old woman glared at the playground. She watched the children play as though planning to eat them all.

Andrés toddled right up to her as if he meant to offer himself as a sacrificial meal to spare the other kids. He stood and stared at the old woman. She stared right back at him. Neither moved or spoke until Gabe swooped in, scooped him up, and gave a quick apology.

The old lady turned her mighty glare on Gabe. He flinched, retreated to the sandy playground, and put Andrés down.

The toddler immediately headed for a trio of girls building sand castles with shovels and buckets. He snatched away one of their shovels when he got there.

"Hey!" the shovel-owner shouted. She seemed old enough to have a sense of ownership, but too young to realize that Andrés didn't. Gabe moved to intercept. Then several things happened very quickly.

Gabe picked up Andrés and plucked the plastic shovel from his hand.

Andrés let out an indignant squawk.

The older boys on the basketball court gave a warning shout.

Their ball flew away from the court in a high arc headed for the middle of the sand castles.

Before it could land and destroy all the sandy buildings in its path, Gabe kicked the ball like a soccer goalie. It sailed away from the kids, away from the castles, and back toward the basketball court. He did this while still holding the squawking Andrés. Then he took a breath and smiled, proud of his reflexes and also a little surprised.

One of the older boys cursed Gabe out for kicking their ball—one shouldn't ever kick a basketball, apparently—and the other grinned and shouted thanks. Gabe waved to both of them as though they had said the same thing, and maybe they had.

He returned the plastic shovel to the castle-building girl, who took it as her rightful due and went back to work. Then Gabe put Andrés down and checked to make sure that Noemi was still under the slide.

She wasn't. She was running away from the playground, downhill and toward the duck pond. She laughed the shrieking laugh of forbidden freedom.

"Your baby sister's making a break for it," Frankie said, helpfully pointing at Noemi but not moving otherwise.

Gabe hoisted Andrés back up again, dropped him into an infant swing to contain him, and sprinted after his sister.

He caught her at the very edge of the pond.

"Splashy!" she yelled while Gabe marched her back up the hill. "Splashy, splashy! Ducks! Duuuuuuuuuuu-uuuuuucks! Meow!"

"Ducks say 'quack,'" Gabe told her.

"Meeeeeooooooow!"

They got back to Andrés, who was trapped in his swing and crying. That set off Noemi, so Gabe pushed them both in the swings for a bit until they cheered up.

"That was smooth," said Frankie, who hadn't budged from his own swing the whole time. "That was ninja-like."

"Thanks," said Gabe. He wanted to point out that Frankie could have helped rather than just sitting there and watching, but he didn't bother.

"I'd still rather be a pirate than a ninja," said Frankie.

They argued about that for a while. It was an old argument between them. Gabe would rather be quiet and precise than boisterous, loud, and sloppy. He preferred throwing stars to cannon fire. But Frankie liked to be loud.

Gabe strapped the twins into their double stroller once they were both laughing and happy. Each seat had a five-point harness, as though the stroller were secretly a space capsule.

"Time to go home," he said. He didn't want to go. The afternoon had suddenly become the very end of Gabe and Frankie's shared summer. But it was still time.

"I guess so," said Frankie.

"You'll have fun in California," said Gabe, trying to put the best spin on it—even though he was still disappointed and grumpy about the whole thing. That rocket-pipe had been a dumb idea all around, but Gabe had gone along, taken the blame for it afterward, and now faced a friendless summer. He shouldn't have let Frankie light that fuse.

"Sure," said Frankie without enthusiasm. "I'll have fun."

They argued about Batman and Zorro while they walked home. Lately they had taken to watching old Batman cartoons and older Zorro cartoons online at Frankie's house. Both cartoon heroes were rich gentlemen who wore masks, hid in caves, and named themselves after stealthy animals—but otherwise they were completely different.

"So which one would win in a fight?" Frankie wanted to know.

"They wouldn't ever get into a fight," said Gabe. He said it quietly, as a known and simple fact.

"But what if they did?" Frankie asked, his voice very much louder.

"They wouldn't fight," Gabe repeated. "It wouldn't happen. It couldn't happen."

"What if they fought by mistake?" Frankie pressed him. "Maybe one of them was framed, or hypnotized, or possessed by evil alien ghosts, or something like that?"

"Zorro would still find a way to avoid it," said Gabe. "Batman would come at him all brooding and serious, and Zorro would just say something charming, or else make him laugh, and then the fight would be over before it even started because you can't crack up laughing and still be Batman. Zorro would make a game out of it."

"If Batman got possessed by aliens, then the aliens wouldn't care about Zorro's sense of humor," Frankie pointed out. "None of Zorro's jokes would make sense to aliens."

"You can't say for sure what would make sense to aliens," said Gabe. "And Zorro would parry anything Batman threw at him. He'd duck and weave and snap batarangs out of the air with his whip. Also, *batarang* is a dumb word. How could anyone who carries a belt full of batarangs take themselves so seriously?"

Frankie's voice got even louder. "I can't hear you over the sound of how wrong you are. It's deafening. Your wrongness."

They stopped at a street corner. Gabe needed to turn left to get home. Frankie's place was off to the right.

"Don't burn anything at your dad's," Gabe told him. "You'll probably start a whole forest fire out there. If I turn on the news and all of California's burning, I'll know it's your fault."

"Don't have fun without me," said Frankie. "No fun."

"I probably won't," said Gabe.

They did their secret handshake, which was complicated. Then both of them went home.

The Envoy moved low to the ground between hedges and trees, still dripping with pond water. Gabe didn't notice it following him.

3

Gabe's house was a duplex. His family rented half of it. No one lived in the other half. The landlord planned to fix it up this summer, but Gabe hadn't seen any sign of him lately. The landlord wasn't really one for fixing things.

Gabe climbed the back steps with a twin under each arm. He nudged open their screen door with his toe and went inside.

His father was in the kitchen, making chicken curry tamales—a fusion of Mexican and Indian cooking—with mango chutney and a mole sauce of his own magnificent invention.

Both of Gabe's parents were *tapatíos*—meaning they came from Guadalajara, Mexico—but they met each other in India. His mother Isabelle was a student at the time. His father Octavio wasn't. He couldn't ever stay in classrooms for long. He spent his time riding a motor-cycle named Baghera across the subcontinent, swapping recipes in every town and working as a chef in exchange for rooms to sleep in. Isabelle studied archeology and went to India to dig around in ancient ruins, even though there were excellent opportunities to dig up ancient ruins without having to leave Mexico—or even go far outside Guadalajara. Her parents had pointed this out to her at the time. She just smiled, nodded, and left anyway. She met Gabe's father on the other side of the world, and they were married by the time they got back.

Now Gabe's dad worked in professional kitchens, but he hated the efficiency that restaurant work required of him. At home he was inefficient. He used as many pots and pans as he possibly could, and changed his mind often about what he was actually cooking. His spice rack—which used to be a bookshelf—took up much of the kitchen. He kept each distinct sort of spice in an unlabeled jam jar and needed four jars to hold all the cumin. Somehow he still knew what was what.

Tonight Gabe's father cooked while singing classic Bollywood tunes.

Gabe strapped each twin into a high chair and buckled their seat belts to prevent escape.

"You've got them?" he asked, passing the child-care

torch to his father and making sure that he noticed it was happening.

His father nodded and set two small bowls of tasty glop aside to cool.

"Yeeeeeeeh dostieeeeeeeee, hum nahieeeeeeeeee todengeeeeeeee," he sang, stirring the various pots that bubbled over the stove. He tested the curry temperature with his pinky finger, found it suitable for toddlers, and set the two bowls on the two high-chair trays. The twins both sank their hands into the thick glop and stuffed their faces.

Gabe grabbed a Coke from the fridge—a *Mexican* Coke, made with cane sugar rather than corn syrup. All the local supermarkets and grocery stores imported Mexican Coca-Cola in small glass bottles. The newer, American stuff tasted like sweetened battery acid. Superior soda in hand, Gabe fled from his father's singing and headed upstairs.

His bedroom contained a bed, a bookshelf, and all three family pets.

Zora the parrot circled Gabe's head a couple of times before landing on it. Then she walked back and forth as though patrolling the top of a medieval tower. Gabe winced as the small claws pricked his scalp, but he didn't brush her off.

Garuda the iguana sat on the bookshelf and looked

Gabe over with one reptilian eyeball. He'd crushed half the city that Gabe had built on that shelf using little plastic bricks. The bricks were a chaotic mixture of several different toy sets, part moon base and part castle and part jungle, inhabited by little plastic characters who were never meant to mix together.

Dad had wanted to name the bird Garuda instead, but Lupe had thought it suited the lizard better because it kind of sounded like Godzilla. Lupe won. Dad still grumbled about it.

Sir Toby the silver fox curled up at the foot of Gabe's bed, pretending to sleep. Gabe could tell by the fox's ears and the squint of his eyes that this was just an act.

The Envoy crept along a tree branch outside and watched through the window. No one noticed it except Garuda, who watched the Envoy sideways with his other stoic eye.

Gabe closed his bedroom door. "Hello, everybody."

"Hello!" said Zora from the top of his head. "Meow!" Noemi had taught her to say "meow," which only reinforced Noemi's belief that "meow" was the proper thing to say to *all* animals—even though there were no cats among the family pets.

Garuda twitched his tail and knocked over more of the plastic city.

Sir Toby made a small yip-snore and kept both eyes closed.

The Envoy said nothing. It curled around the tree branch and listened from outside.

All three pets were refugees, abandoned and given shelter in Gabe's house. They used to belong to various neighbors, but they had stayed when their former families moved away.

"We'll just watch them until we can find better homes for them," Gabe's father had said each time. No one believed him, and no one in the family had ever tried to find those alternate homes.

Zora flew from Gabe's head to Sir Toby's haunch. The fox swiveled his huge ears and opened one eye, which looked like a little sphere of frozen ink. The bird walked up and down his spine. The fox closed his eyes and stretched, enjoying the bird-foot massage.

Gabe sat on the floor. There wasn't very much floor. His bed took up most of the space.

Sir Toby made a yip-grumble at Zora, no longer enjoying his bird-foot massage. She didn't seem to notice. Gabe reached over, dislodged the bird, and then pretended to sneeze. She sneezed back at him. Fake sneezes were her favorite noise to make.

"Food!" Dad shouted from the bottom of the stairs.

Gabe left his door open, just in case any of the pets wanted to leave, and went back downstairs.

Mom came home just as Dad set the kitchen table. They all talked about nothing much in Spanish, English, and Spanglish.

Lupe, the eldest, came in late with apologies. She wore all black, as befitting a waitress. Her place at the table was already set. She slid smoothly into her chair, and smoothly into the conversation. Her full name was Guadalupe, but she never used it. She never liked it much, even though it sort of meant "River of the Wolf," which Gabe thought was unspeakably cool. She had been born on their grandmother Guadalupe's birthday, so she couldn't avoid inheriting that name.

The Envoy watched them all from inside a cupboard. It had squeezed through mouse-chewed holes in the walls to get there. It watched, listened, and paid particular attention to Gabe—and it noticed how Gabe paid attention to everyone.

Gabe's mother shifted her posture, suddenly tense. She stared at the food as though trying to scry the future in it.

Lupe looked for the salt. She loved salt. But it always annoyed Dad to add any salt to his already perfectly balanced collage of flavors, so she didn't actually ask for the salt. Gabe noticed anyway and passed her the salt-shaker. It was shaped like an Olmec statue head with a great big helmet. Both the salt- and pepper shakers were cheap gifts from Gabe's grandparents—reminders to his mother that she could just come home to study ancient civilizations if she still wanted to be an archeologist.

Gabe thought the helmeted heads looked like astro-nauts. Mom said they were probably ancient ballplayers, and she insisted, firmly and often, that they were not astronauts.

Gabe made sure that Dad wasn't looking when he passed the salt to Lupe. Dad and Lupe loved to argue about anything and everything, but Dad took actual offense where his cooking was concerned.

Little Andrés dropped his spoon and started fussing, even though he never actually used the spoon to eat with. He still wanted it back. No one noticed but Gabe, so Gabe picked up the spoon, wiped it off, and gave it back to his little brother.

"I need to run errands tomorrow," Mom said, still watching her food more than eating it. "You don't have a shift in the morning, do you?" she asked Dad.

"Not until noon," he said around a mouthful of curry.

"Good," said Mom. "I'll need your help lifting things. I can drop you off afterward."

"I could help," said Lupe.

"No," said Mom. The word was a high fence tossed up between them. "Summer classes start tomorrow. Remember?"

Lupe started to say something angry and dismissive, stopped, started to say something else, and then stuffed her mouth to keep herself from saying anything.

Gabe wasn't sure why his mother and sister caught fire every single time they spoke. He just wished they would stop. The two of them did *not* love to argue, not with each other, but lately they couldn't seem to help it.

He asked for something that he knew he couldn't have and didn't actually want. "Can you drop me off at Minnehaha Park tomorrow morning? The one with the waterfall? I have to write about it for a summer reading project."

Lupe gave a snort of disgust. Now. she would be annoyed with him for acting like such a perfect little student—which was strange, since she used to be a perfect student herself—but Gabe could live with that. She didn't catch on fire when she was annoyed with Gabe.

Mom shook her head. "No room for all of us in the car, not with both car seats." She finally started to eat her curry, but she still made grunting, subvocalized noises.

"I told you we should have traded the car in for that minivan," Dad said.

"That van was embarrassed and embarrassing," Lupe protested. "It was so rusted out that it would've fallen to pieces in shame just as soon as anybody said something mean to it."

"I could have fixed it," said Dad.

"You can't actually fix cars," said Lupe. "I know you feel like you *should* be able to, but you can't. It never works out."

"I fixed old Baghera so many times—"

"A motorcycle is not a minivan!"

Gabe sat back, relieved. This was something that Dad and Lupe *enjoyed* arguing about, and the topic wouldn't wound either one of them. They fought without fire.

"Just take the bus to the park," Mom told Gabe, ignoring the minivan argument. "You can manage that by yourself. You're the most sensible member of this whole family. You're the only one who knows how to keep your head down."

"Even though he's the only one who doesn't *need* to," Lupe muttered.

Mom said nothing, loudly.

Gabe wondered what Lupe meant. He decided not to care. Instead he tried to think of a way to distract them from another argument, but he didn't have to, because the twins started blowing raspberries at each other and that was adorable. Everyone paid attention to the twins and seemed to forget about the ire that crackled between Lupe and Mom.

The Fuentes family finished their meal.

4

Gabe turned out his light, climbed into bed, and found the flashlight he had stashed behind the mattress. He read a bit of *Hiawatha* for his summer reading project, read of "days that are forgotten, in the unremembered ages," but the *THUMP thump THUMP thump* beat made him immediately sleepy. He read the lines "Break the red stone from this quarry, Mould and make it into Peace-Pipes," at least three times, his eyes sliding over them and finding no traction. He wanted to enjoy it, but the book would have to wait for daylight.

He set *Hiawatha* aside, picked up an old favorite instead, opened the book at random, and reread one of the chapters in the middle. He liked to do this with books he'd read already, liked to leap into the middle of things and let himself remember the rest of the story in both directions—all the stuff that had already happened and everything still to come, everything he knew that the characters didn't yet.

Sir Toby climbed out from under the bed and sniffed the air a few times, suspicious. Then he jumped into bed and curled up at Gabe's feet.

Garuda climbed down from the bookshelf and clawed his way up the blankets to settle next to the fox and enjoy mammalian warmth.

Zora slept in her covered cage in the corner. The cage moved from room to room, and tonight Gabe had moved it in with him. He was still annoyed to be facing a Frankie-free summer, and felt better keeping all three pets close.

The Envoy oozed through a heating grate in the floor. It shaped part of itself into a mouth and throat, and then cleared its new throat with a thick, phlegmy sound.

Gabe and Sir Toby both sat up at the odd noise. The fox jumped to the floor. Gabe swung his flashlight beam around and found the Envoy.

The purple, transparent thing on the floor of his room flinched away from the flashlight beam and became slightly less transparent. Then it spoke.

"I am the Envoy." It changed shape slightly to adjust the sound of its voice. "I'm the Envoy," it said again. It sounded nervous. It also sounded just like Gabe's mother.

"Messenger. Traveler with important news. One who knows what others need to learn. I have no other name than Envoy. Hello. Hi, there."

Gabe tried to say something but failed to say anything. His stare was a question mark a thousand miles high.

Sir Toby approached, his tail bristled and his ears pressed back like a cat's.

The Envoy lowered its mouth to be sniffed.

Sir Toby made a challenging and inquisitive yip-bark.

The Envoy changed the shape of its throat and gave a few yips of its own.

Sir Toby relaxed. His tail settled down and his ears perked up, as though recognizing those noises to mean, *Thanks for letting me trespass on your territory,* and also, *I'm not going to bite you. I don't even have any teeth to bite you with, and I recognize that your teeth are impressive. Your coat and your tail are also impressive.* Maybe they did. Those were the sorts of things Gabe would have wanted to say to Sir Toby, if only he spoke fox.

The Envoy changed shape again, took a breath, and made air into words.

"Hello," it said again. "Greetings to you. Welcome. No, wait. I mean that I'm asking for your welcome and attention rather than offering you welcome. This is your home, so it's not my role to be welcoming."

"You sound like my mom," Gabe whispered. "You look like a purple sock puppet without any eyes glued on, though I can see right through you, and there's no hand inside to make the mouth move. And you sound like my mom."

The Envoy nodded. "I have mimicked the shape of her vocal cords so that I can talk to you in a pleasingly familiar way. Is it working?"

"Not really," said Gabe. "Nothing about this is pleasingly familiar."

The Envoy took another breath to use as word-fuel. It still sounded nervous. It started to babble.

"My purpose is to assist ambassadors. But this world has been without an ambassador for many years, and it very much needs one, so now it's my purpose to select one. I have traveled very far, most recently from the moon—the only moon you have left—to select a new ambassador. The word *ambassador* means one who speaks on behalf of a place and people in dialogue and diplomacy with other peoples and places. Proxy. Diplomat. Representative and plenipotentiary."

Gabe blinked a few times. "I know what *ambassador* means."

"Excellent," said the Envoy. "That's excellent."

"I'm not sure about *plenipotentiary*, though."

"It also means *ambassador*," the Envoy explained.

"I figured that it probably did," said Gabe.

"And I have selected you to take this post," said the Envoy.

"Me," said Gabe. "Ambassador. One who speaks on behalf of a place and people."

"Yes," said the Envoy. "Your world, in this case. Your planet."

"Then who are you asking me to speak *to*?"

"Everyone else," said the Envoy.

Gabe looked up. He couldn't help looking up, even though his view of the night sky was blocked by the ceiling of his room, the roof of his house, and urban light pollution that turned the sky into a dusky, starless place.

Gabe set his flashlight on the floor, pointing up, to serve as a dim bedside lamp. "Okay. I'm flattered. But I'm also *eleven*. Aliens I can accept—mostly because there's one in my room—but not an eleven-year-old ambassador."

"I'm not actually alien to this world," the Envoy said. It became more transparent now that the flashlight beam no longer shone on it directly. "Not quite. Not precisely. And I'd have guessed that you were younger than eleven. The previous ambassador was younger."

"Younger?" Gabe laughed. "Somebody *younger* than me represented this whole planet?"

The Envoy grinned an odd-looking and puppet-like grin. "Good! You laughed. That's an excellent sign. You feel comfortable enough to laugh. And, yes, people younger than you have served as ambassadors. For very good reasons." It pointed its mouth at the fox and iguana. "The mammal and the lizard there. Are they friendly to each other? Sociable?"

"Yes . . ." said Gabe, clearly unsure where this conversational turn might be going.

"Then they probably met while very young—at least while one of them was very young. Is that the case?"

Gabe nodded. "The fox was a little cub when we took him in. The family just across the street bought him, but their cats didn't like him, so they ditched him right away. He was tiny."

"*That* is why the two are friendly, though they're such different species. Juveniles have not yet fixed the boundaries of their social world. They haven't drawn a circle around those worth talking to. Adults of most species find it more difficult to communicate with anyone outside their arbitrary circle—or even recognize that anybody exists outside it. So ambassadors are always young. Always."

Sir Toby jumped back up on the bed and yawned, apparently satisfied that the Envoy was safe enough to ignore. Garuda woke up. The two of them bumped noses and then both went back to sleep.

"Okay," said Gabe. "Sure. But why choose me? I just destroyed a lot of lawn furniture with a toy rocket. It was Frankie's fault, really, but I couldn't stop him. I shouldn't represent anybody. I definitely shouldn't represent *everybody*."

The Envoy smiled again with its puppet-like mouth. "I find your doubts encouraging. Anyone who agrees to take this on without first giving the task some serious thought would probably be a terrible ambassador. And I admit that I've selected you partly by accident. I fell into your neighborhood, though I wasn't really aiming for it. I was only aiming for the planet. But I've spent days observing children in the park. You are the only one I decided to follow. You can settle disputes. You treat other species respectfully, as members of your immediate family, despite differences in perception and cognition. And the two of us can have this conversation at all. Even though myself and my message are both unexpected and strange, you can set aside your shock and actually talk about this. Not everyone can do that. For all these reasons I've selected you as suitable for the post."

Gabe sat up a little straighter. He clearly didn't mind the compliments.

"Would I have to leave home?" he asked. "Mom wouldn't be able to keep her tutoring jobs if she didn't have me around to babysit sometimes."

"Good!" the Envoy said. "You immediately think about how your choices might affect those around you. This is how an ambassador should always think. And, no, you wouldn't have to leave home. Your ambassadorship will involve diplomatic communication with the delegates of other worlds, but you can accomplish this from here. And we'll work together in secret if we can. Human governments dislike knowing about things beyond their control. They find it frustrating and often exercise their frustrations on the ambassadors themselves. I've found that stealth works better, with your species at least."

Gabe nodded, still thoughtful, still mulling over so much new information.

"Yes," he said. "I *have* to say yes. I get to talk to aliens. I don't think I really could say anything other than yes."

"Excellent," said the Envoy. "Now, do you have any sodium bicarbonate in your kitchen?"

"What?" Gabe asked.

"Baking soda," the Envoy clarified.

"Probably," said Gabe. "Definitely. Sure."

"I lost a substantial amount of mass when I fell," the Envoy explained. "The experience was exciting, but it was also scalding and dehydrating. I still need more nutrients to rebuild the lost substance of myself."

"Sure," said Gabe.

He climbed out of bed. The lizard and the silver fox looked up, and then both of them went back to sleep.

Gabe left his room and crept downstairs. The Envoy followed, oozing down the steps like a slow, purple waterfall.

5

Gabe took a box of baking soda from the back of the fridge and a glass of water from the sink. He set them both on the kitchen floor.

The Envoy scooted up to the glass, reached out with its puppetish appendage, and used it as a hand to pick up the drink. The rest of its body changed shape, becoming bowl-like. It poured the water into the bowl of itself and dumped the baking soda in after it. The mixture bubbled and fizzed while the Envoy's skin absorbed it all.

"Is that better?" Gabe asked.

The Envoy changed shape again to breathe and speak. The lump of baking soda still visibly fizzed in the middle of it. "Much better," it said. "Thank you."

Gabe sat on the floor. It seemed more companionable than sitting high up at the kitchen table. The Envoy went on fizzing.

"How do ambassadors talk to each other?" Gabe asked. "Nobody's ever answered our radio signals."

"Radio signals are slow," the Envoy said. "No, that's not true at all. Radio signals are very fast and travel just as quickly as light does. But the closest solar system is four light-years away, so light takes four local years to get there. If you wanted to have a talk with someone in that system, and both of you used radios, then that conversation would take too long. 'Hello?' you might start out saying. 'Hello!' they might answer, and already eight years are gone by the time you hear their answer. Ambassadors should be young—or at least *neotenous*—and at that rate you'd be very old before you finished with introductory small talk. Ambassadors must also have dealings with worlds very much farther away, hundreds and thousands of light-years distant. We don't have time to wait hundreds and thousands of years between one 'hello' and another, so we never bother to use such things as radio."

"What does *neotenous* mean?" Gabe asked.

"Species who keep childish traits in adulthood are neotenous," the Envoy said. "Curiosity, the ability to learn new things and form new social connections—these are neotenous traits. Some humans are like this. Others become grumpy, solitary, and inflexible as they get older."

"Got it," said Gabe. He mulled over the definition for

a bit. "So how do we talk to each other if the speed of light is still too slow?"

"Nothing travels faster than light," the Envoy said. "Nothing but the Machinae, and I don't know how they manage it." It grinned its wide and unsettling grin. "But some dimensions curl in over each other, such that everything within them exists at a single point with no space in between. There are places where that first Big Bang never banged, where all things are still very close together, and *that's* where communication bounces between worlds. That's where it can be entangled such that there's no actual distance for it to travel through."

Gabe stared at the Envoy and the fizzing baking soda inside it.

"Did that make sense to you?" the Envoy asked.

"It *sounded* like it made sense," Gabe said carefully. "I'd like to just pretend that it did and move on. Maybe it'll sink in later."

The Envoy changed color, rapidly alternating between shades of purple. This meant that it felt impatient—not with Gabe but with itself. "Let me show you the basement. I can explain this better if first I show you the basement."

"Why?" Gabe asked. "What's in the basement?"

"I spent hours down there waiting for the chance

to talk to you," the Envoy said. "While I waited, I dismantled and repurposed much of the machinery I found."

"You did *what*?"

"Come see." The Envoy oozed out of the room.

Gabe warily followed it down to the basement, where he stood and gaped at the state of things.

The Envoy had taken apart the dryer and washing machine, rebuilt both at opposite ends of the room, and combined them with parts from a broken television. None of these things actually belonged to Gabe's family. The landlord would be annoyed.

"I've built a device of entanglement for you!" the Envoy announced in a triumphant way. "I've done this many times before for every ambassador, improvising with different materials each time. Usually it takes longer than just a few hours to build—especially underwater—but I've become very good at it."

Gabe took a step toward the mess of spinning and humming machinery. "You've had to build these underwater?"

"Oh yes," the Envoy said. "I selected many aquatic ambassadors before your species emerged and learned how to talk to each other. And the best physicists on this world are often squid. You notice things about light underwater that take longer to notice otherwise. Have you ever read squid poetry? It doesn't last long. The ink quickly disperses into the surrounding water. But it's beautiful poetry once you learn how to read it."

"What's that glow?" Gabe asked, pointing. A speck of gold light flickered inside the washer. An identical speck flickered in the dryer several feet away.

"That light is the same in these two separate places," the Envoy told him, excited and proud. "They are entangled across the distance of your basement. What happens to one will also happen to the other at the very same moment with no lag of travel between them."

"So I can use it to send instant messages," Gabe said. He sounded disappointed. "Ambassadors don't ever meet in person? Visit each other's planets, that sort of thing?"

"Not so often," the Envoy admitted. "Travel is much more difficult than communication. But you should know that there are strange ships in this solar system already."

"What?" Gabe asked, unsure if he'd heard that right. "Really? Who are they?"

"I don't know," said the Envoy. "I wish I did. I spotted them from the moon, using abandoned equipment I'd been tinkering with there. The ships are hiding in the asteroid belt between Jupiter and Mars. It worried me. I found it inauspicious, inopportune, and distressing to see vehicles from elsewhere when we have no ambassador to talk to them. So I came looking for one and found you. This means that you're likely to engage in some unusual, in-person diplomacy. I hope it goes well."

That sounded ominous. Gabe glanced at the Envoy, who quickly raised both its voice and its neck. "Besides all that, entanglement will allow you to send more than just messages! You can send yourself, which is almost like meeting in person. You can entangle your perceptions. In this way you will dream yourself into the Embassy where all other ambassadors gather."

"I'll be able to dream about meeting aliens?" Gabe asked, skeptical.

"You won't just dream *about* meeting aliens," the Envoy clarified. "You will experience the actual facts of such meetings in dreams. But first I have to do a little more tinkering and adjust the field of recoherence." It moved across the concrete floor, picked up a few metal pieces of washing machine, and swallowed them.

"Still hungry?" Gabe asked. "I can probably find you more baking soda."

The Envoy shook its mouth. "I'm sustained, thank you," it said. "I'm partially digesting these metals in order to shift their molecules into more useful combinations, and not because I'm hungry."

"Oh," said Gabe. He sat on the basement steps and

watched, fascinated, while the metal pieces changed color inside the Envoy. It pushed them out, added them to the device of entanglement, and absorbed other pieces to work strange changes on. Then it took a breath and shifted to keep the pocket of air separate from the floating pieces of metal.

"This is we how we will entangle you," it said. "First we'll embed tiny particles inside you—most especially in the skin of your eyelids, the surface of your eardrums, and all along your spine. Then we will entangle those particles and propel their identical twins through the tiny black hole I will make in your clothes dryer."

"You can make a black hole in the dryer?"

"Yes," said the Envoy. "Please do not stand too close to it."

"Can I throw something at it and watch what happens?" Gabe asked.

"No," said the Envoy. "It will be very precisely calibrated."

"Not even little scraps of paper or balls of dryer lint or something like that?"

The Envoy cleared its long, purple throat. "Please do not throw anything at the black hole! Accounting for the air and dust motes is hard enough. It will remember everything it absorbs. We have to sneak the particles of your entanglement through that attention, avoiding its notice. Once the entangled particles pass through the black hole, they'll travel between the ninth and tenth dimensions of our universe, skim across the surface of an adjacent universe, shift in and out of places where neither space nor distance currently exist, and finally arrive at the Embassy. You might have some very strange dreams before they arrive. Try not to be alarmed by your dreams."

"Okay," said Gabe. "I'll try. I never really remember my dreams anyway."

"You'll remember these," the Envoy said. "Once the particles reach the Embassy, they'll form a precisely entangled duplicate of your perception and awareness. You'll see, hear, and move as though actually there, even though the Embassy is twenty-five thousand light-years away in the very center of the galaxy."

"I thought there was a really big black hole at the center of the galaxy," said Gabe. He was the sort of kid who knew such things.

"There is," said the Envoy. "The Embassy is perched on the very edge." It added molecularly modified pieces of dryer to the rest of the device. "We're ready to begin. The device is ready, at least. Are you ready?"

"Will it hurt?" Gabe asked, though he didn't feel worried.

"Not very much," the Envoy said.

Gabe felt a bit worried now. "Is it safe?" he pressed.

"No," said the Envoy. "Definitely not. Nothing is safe. Neither food nor playgrounds nor standing where meteors might land on you—which is anywhere and everywhere—is ever safe. There's no such quality as safe. Instead there is trust. We've only just met, you and I, so I understand if we don't yet have enough trust between us. We can delay your entanglement. But if you wish to accept this post to help protect your world and every form of life residing on it, then you must become entangled. And given that we have strange ships in the asteroid belt, I really do encourage you to hurry."

Gabe looked from one small golden glow to the other. "You can do this entanglement thing without making my head explode?"

"Certainly," the Envoy said. "I've never yet exploded the head of an ambassador."

"Okay," said Gabe. "Okay," he said again. "I'll need you to rebuild the washer and dryer soon anyway. The twins go through lots of laundry. Our old washing machine broke right after they were born, and it took the landlord forever to replace it, so Lupe and I had to carry wagonloads of crap-stained onesies to the Laundromat almost every single day. So let's do this quickly."

"Are you certain?" the Envoy asked.

"No," said Gabe. "Hurry up."

The Envoy paused. "We should conduct your entanglement with a little more ceremony and reverence for a very long tradition."

Gabe laughed. "I accept the role of ambassador with all due formality, because my little sister and brother are going to need clothes that aren't covered in poop."

The Envoy sighed. "Please stand over here."

Gabe stood over there.

The Envoy scootched behind the former washing machine and made adjustments. The flickering light inside the dryer vanished. Gabe squinted at where it used to be. He couldn't see inside the dryer. No light escaped the dryer to see by.

"Repeat after me," the Envoy said. "I will speak for this world."

"I will speak for this world," said Gabriel Sandro Fuentes.

"Now close your eyes," the Envoy told him. "You'll feel a tingling sensation in your eyelids, eardrums, and all along your spine."

Gabe closed his eyes.

He still saw a blinding flash of light.

PART TWO
ENTANGLED

6

Gabe never remembered his dreams. When other people talked about the bizarre, wonderful, or horrifying things they saw and did while sleeping, Gabe had always just listened and wondered what that would be like.

His sister Lupe had a recurring dream about migrating birds who were also words. Sometimes they made messages on the undersides of storm clouds. Lupe never remembered the messages in the morning, but at least she remembered the rest of the dream.

Frankie described his dreams at length and often, even the ones that made no sense. Especially the ones that made no sense. "And then I was an eggplant and somehow I'd climbed onto the roof even though I didn't have arms, though I think maybe I still had legs at that point, and one of the trees in the backyard was also my mom and she forced me to play card games, but I'd forgotten how to play all of them, and I tried to explain to her how I'd forgotten, but she really wasn't listening so . . ." Then Frankie and Gabe would play card games just to reassure Frankie that he really did remember how. Sometimes Gabe would win, and sometimes Gabe would let Frankie win if he figured that Frankie needed to win at something.

Gabe was pretty sure that he had dreams just like everyone else, and sometimes he could just barely glimpse one as it vanished in the very first moments of the morning, but he couldn't ever hold it. Before entanglement, Gabe's dreams left no footprints or bread crumbs in his memory.

After entanglement, Ambassador Gabriel Sandro Fuentes remembered *all* his dreams—almost. He remembered all of them but one.

That first night he dreamed about motion and travel somewhere on the other side of the tiny black hole in his basement. He skipped and burrowed through the substance of nothing while stars stood fixed around him and watched him from very far away. Gabe tried to close his eyes in the dream, but he couldn't. He hadn't brought his eyelids with him.

Suddenly and without warning he stood alone outside his house, in the center of the street. He was still in motion. He still saw stars in every direction. But he was also stuck in the road, unable to move out of the way if a car came hurtling over the asphalt.

Zora and Garuda walked by, the iguana in a top hat and the bird in an evening gown. They greeted him in Spanish. Gabe realized that he had forgotten his Spanish, the language that was supposed to be his own. He felt a heavy shame that anchored him more firmly to the middle of the street.

The light around him twisted, burned, and shriveled. His entangled senses passed through solar storms between twin suns. He woke up sweating.

Lupe pounded on his bedroom door.

"Wake up, wake up, wake up!" his sister said. "Dad wants you at breakfast."

"I'm up," Gabe mumbled.

He closed his eyes. He could still see solar storms behind his eyelids. The dream wasn't evaporating the way his dreams usually did.

Lupe pounded on the door again.

"I'm up!" Gabe said, louder this time.

He got up. He got dressed. He checked in with the Envoy, who occupied an otherwise empty aquarium in Gabe's closet.

"Morning, Envoy."

The Envoy's mouth peered up from the aquarium

like a purple periscope. It made a throat for itself and cleared it. "Good morning, Ambassador. How do you feel? How's your head? Does it ache? Is it dizzy? I see that it hasn't exploded."

"Nope," said Gabe. "Still here. No headaches, no dizziness. No explosions."

"Good," said the Envoy.

"I think so too," said Gabe. "I did have a weird dream, though."

"Did you arrive at the Embassy in this dream?" the Envoy asked, alert and more interested.

"No," said Gabe. "But how will I know?"

"You'll know," said the Envoy. "Protocol will welcome you when you arrive. I should explain more before you actually get there. And once there, you should try to learn whose ships are nearby."

"Okay," said Gabe. He yawned. "So what's Protocol, exactly?"

Someone knocked on his bedroom door. The Envoy ducked its mouth back into the aquarium, and Gabe shut the closet. "Hello?"

His mother came in, looked around at the floor, and suggested that she might be going insane. "I've lost some laundry," she said. "I was sure I put in a load this morning, very first thing, but now it's gone. Poof. I've looked everywhere. You didn't helpfully empty the dryer and then put all the clothes away, did you?"

Gabe heard a burbling and unhappy noise come through his closet door.

"No . . . ," said Gabe.

"Ai," she said. "Well, hurry downstairs. Your father is waiting to fry up your breakfast."

"I'll be right there." Gabe promised.

Mom went downstairs.

Gabe opened the closet. "Did you hear that? A load of laundry disappeared."

"That shouldn't have happened," the Envoy said, sounding nervous. It climbed out of the aquarium. "The black hole should have dissipated completely by now. I'll go back to the basement. Hopefully the basement still exists. Don't let anyone else go down there." It oozed out of the room through a heating grate.

Now Gabe felt extremely awake. He dashed through the house, confirmed the non-basement location of every family member, and gathered up all three pets, locking them in his room. Then, and only then, Gabe got dressed, brushed his teeth, and joined his father in the kitchen.

Dad gave him a nod, tossed bread dough in a pan of oil, and handed Gabe a cup of homemade *horchata*. Then he poured himself a cup of coffee. It was probably his third cup of the morning. He wore an old cooking apron composed of more grease than fabric and covered in whole constellations of splattered stains.

Gabe sat and sipped his sweet-but-not-too-sweet *horchata*. He thought about his dream, rolled it over and over in his head the way he might roll an unfamiliar taste around in his mouth. He still remembered it, all of it, from solar wind to silly top hat.

Dad called Lupe into the room. Then he set a plate of fried bread with two spoonfuls of greasy, salty garbanzo beans in front of Gabe. It smelled like greasy, salty poetry.

Lupe joined them. She wore a black T-shirt with a sparkling pink Superman symbol on the front. She looked impatient. She usually did.

Dad sat down across the table and folded both hands in front of him. "It is time once again to go over the family emergency plans."

Gabe and Lupe groaned.

"Shush," said Dad.

He did this often. Dad had emergency plans for fire, flood, tornado, car accident, and the sudden disappearance of family members. He had *several* plans for sudden disappearances. He went through them all, point by point, and quizzed his eldest children on each. He inquired after the location and contents of their jump bags—backpacks stuffed with emergency changes of clothes, cash, snacks, and other supplies. They wouldn't need to pack first if they ever had to leave the house in a hurry.

After that Dad proceeded to the silly plans, though he still went through them with the utmost seriousness. Most involved ghosts. Gabe's father liked ghost stories. He had plans for wailing ghosts, ghosts wearing veils, and ghosts wandering back and forth near ponds, lakes, or the river. He had plans for pirate ghosts, ghosts in mirrors, and ghosts throwing things in the kitchen. He insisted that he had trapped one such spirit in an empty olive jar. "It liked to toss my knives around at night," he warned them. "Don't you dare open the olive jar in the very back of the cupboard."

Most of the ghost plans fit into the "evacuate immediately" category, though some of them suggested appeasement: find out what the ghost wants and try to give it to them. If the ghost happened to be trapped in an endless, painful, post-traumatic, post-mortal loop and couldn't stop reenacting the way that it died, then Dad suggested breaking the loop by distracting the ghost somehow. Possible methods of distraction included loud *norteño* music, which no one in the family actually liked.

Gabe noticed for the first time that they had no alien-related plans. He wondered how Mom would react to the suggestion that they plan for aliens, given that she kind of hated science fiction. He also wondered what she would think of his new job. He picked up the saltshaker and then put it down again.

A strange, metallic shriek came from the basement.

"What was that?" Lupe asked. "That sounded spooky. Should we initiate the plan for basement hauntings?"

Dad stood up to investigate.

"I'll go," Gabe quickly volunteered, and ran out of the kitchen.

He opened the basement door, half-expecting the staircase to swallow him whole.

It didn't. The light was on. Gabe was relieved to see that the basement still existed and that light could still escape it. He went halfway down the stairs and peered over the handrail.

The Envoy sat on top of the half-dismantled dryer with a wrench in its mouth. It had built a wire frame around the appliance with dozens of coat hangers.

"Shhhhh," Gabe whispered.

The Envoy swallowed the wrench.

"Apologies," it whispered. Then it spit the wrench back out and returned to work.

Gabe went back to the kitchen table and shrugged. "No ghosts."

He ate another helping of spicy garbanzos while they finished going over emergency ghost plans.

"One more thing," Dad said. He brought out a box, set it on the table, and removed two cloth-wrapped objects from inside. The shorter of the two he gave to Gabe.

"This," he said with solemnity, "is a *vajra* hammer."

Gabe unwrapped the cloth and examined the hammer.

"That," said Lupe with tickled scorn, "is a rubber mallet with strings of beads glued on."

Dad looked annoyed. *"This,"* he repeated, with even more solemnity, "is a *vajra* hammer. In Tibet and India it represents wisdom and the power to smash deceptions and falsehoods. Use it well, Son."

"Thank you, Father," said Gabe with equal ceremony. He shook his new hammer of wisdom and truth to make the beads rattle.

Dad gave the other bundle of cloth to Lupe. "Take this, my firstborn, and keep it safe. It is an important heirloom of our family."

She took it, barely humoring him. "I'm sure it's been an heirloom since you glued it together earlier this morning, whatever it is."

Dad stood back and crossed his arms over his stained apron. He didn't look annoyed. He looked even more smug. "Unwrap it, wiseass."

Lupe removed the cloth to reveal a walking cane of polished wood, capped with a silver handle. Sarcasm fell away from her face in small pieces. She tugged on the silver end and unsheathed a long sword blade.

"That was my grandfather's," Dad said. "Toledo steel, with a seascape etched along the blade. Whenever he had his afternoon nap, I would sneak in, swipe it, and swing it around in the backyard. I always put it back before he woke up."

"Toledo, Ohio?" Lupe asked. She stared at the blade, dazzled. There wasn't as much joke in her voice as she probably meant to put there.

"No, wiseass. Toledo, Spain—the nation of our ancestors. Half of our ancestors anyway. Those who crossed the wide ocean to do horrible things to the other half of our ancestors. Now pay attention. You're the oldest, and the fighter in the family. You keep it safe. Your brother is the diplomat, so I have judged him worthy of a vajra hammer."

That made Gabe nervous. *How did he know that I'm a diplomat? Did he overhear us last night? Or is he just trying to make me feel better about giving me a rubber hammer with beads glued on rather than my great-grandfather's sword?*

Dad gathered up the breakfast plates and dropped

them in the dishwasher. "Take care of these gifts, my children."

"Thanks, Dad," they both said together.

"And, Lupe, you're going to class this morning. Don't give your mother any more grief about summer school."

Lupe started to say something, stopped, and then said something else. "Can I bring the sword?"

"No," said Dad.

After the gift-giving ceremony was over, Mom and the twins moved through the kitchen in a sudden, frenzied bustle of kisses and shouts of "meow." Then Mom and Dad and Noemi and Andrés all left to run errands.

"Make sure your sister goes to class today, my heart," Mom whispered to Gabe on her way out the door. "Make *sure* she does." Gabe promised that he would, insomuch as he could ever influence what Lupe did.

Soon Gabe and Lupe stood alone in the kitchen.

"Can I borrow your hammer?" Lupe asked. "Temporary trade?"

Gabe wasn't sure she was serious. He didn't want to agree too quickly, even though his answer was obviously yes. "Why?"

"Because I have spiders in my room," she told him. "I want to use the mallet of truth and wisdom to convince them that their spidery lives are illusory. If I use the sword to do it, then I'll just make holes in the walls and ceiling. After I smash spiders, I guess I'll go to summer school. After that I have a restaurant shift, so I probably won't see you for the rest of the day. Have fun while I'm gone. Swing that sword around in the backyard if you can do it without hurting yourself—or hurting the sword. Call my cell if you need anything."

Gabe was relieved that he didn't have to try to convince her to leave the house and get far away from the dangerous physics in the basement.

"Why do you need summer school, anyway?" he asked. It felt safer to ask now that Mom wasn't home.

"Because I failed a bunch of classes last year," Lupe told him in a very matter-of-fact sort of way.

Lupe's failed classes did not bother Gabe. What bothered Gabe was that they didn't seem to bother Lupe. "You used to freak out if you got an A-minus."

"I know," she said.

"So what changed?" Gabe asked.

"Just gimme the hammer," she said without answering, making it clear that she wouldn't answer.

He took the cane and gave her the hammer.

She went up to her room to smash spiders.

Gabe checked on the Envoy downstairs. He felt better prepared for whatever he might find now that he carried an ancient weapon of his family—even though he knew that he couldn't defend himself against a black hole with a sword.

The Envoy worked furiously. Red sparks flew from the wire frame. But nothing caught fire or exploded or imploded. The Envoy waved him away with a temporary limb when Gabe tried to ask questions.

He went in the backyard to swing the sword around and enjoy the sound it made. He didn't do that for long, though. He still felt groggy and zombified, like a flu or a fever might be creeping up on him. He saw stars in shadows, and more stars behind his eyelids.

Gabe went upstairs and apologized to the antsy menagerie of pets for their confinement. Then he flopped back onto his bed, even though it was still morning. The three animals roamed the room around him. He could hear the thump of Lupe killing spiders. Despite all this, he quickly fell asleep.

Once asleep, he was elsewhere.

A deep, slow voice announced his arrival.

"The Honorable Gabriel Sandro Fuentes, ambassador of Terra and representative of all Terran life, be welcome."

7

Gabe stood in a small and narrow room, alone. The walls seemed to be made out of thick, smoky glass. He looked up. If this place had a ceiling, it was very far above him.

Hello? he tried to say, but he couldn't speak.

"Be welcome, Ambassador," the room said again in its slow, deep voice. The voice had no accent that Gabe could place. He wasn't even sure what language it spoke. At first he thought it was English, the official and semi-formal English of gray-haired news anchors on television. But it might have been Spanish, the stately Spanish his grandparents always used on the phone when they wanted to seem especially grandparental.

The wall in front of him shifted, becoming silvery and reflective.

"Please observe your own image until it is familiar to

you," the room said. "We are now coordinating the recoherence of your entangled self."

The first thing Gabe saw in the mirror was a floating
metal ball.

Doesn't look much like me so far, he thought.

"Please be patient while you coalesce," the room said.

Now the mirror image looked like a floating tadpole
the size of a soccer ball. It shifted again, growing limbs
and losing a tail, then growing bristly hair before losing
that, too. Throughout each shift the reflection looked
back at Gabe with wide, dark eyes. They were expressive
eyes, full of the same wary, skeptical wonder that Gabe
felt while watching.

"Still not me," he said—out loud, this time. The beastly-
looking thing in the mirror moved its mouth while he
spoke.

"Your remote is collating sense memories," the room
explained. "Some of these memories are very old. Please
be patient. Please do not fidget."

"Sorry." Gabe had been flapping his arms to see what
his reflection would do with its own momentary limbs.
He stopped. "Is this the Embassy?"

"Yes," said the room. It sounded distracted, as though
concentrating on something else.

"Good," said Gabe. "Just glad I'm in the right place.

Hello." He checked out the size and shape of his reflection's teeth.

"Hello," said the room. "I am Protocol. Your remote is very nearly calibrated to your own sense of self."

"That still doesn't quite look like me," said Gabe, scrutinizing his reflection. He wore a simple, reddish robe that looked a little bit like a martial arts uniform. "Close, but too tall."

"Variation and mutations of perception and meaning are unavoidable in translation," said Protocol, sounding annoyed. "Please proceed to the Chancery."

The mirrored wall slid open.

Gabe hadn't actually understood most of that, but it was easy enough to understand the invitation of an open door. He paused in the doorway and peered down the corridor on the other side. He felt air on his skin, a little colder than comfortable. He also felt like he actually had a body here, like his arms and legs were with him. His emotions were a mix of top-of-the-roller-coaster feeling (Gabe didn't actually *like* roller coasters, but he always rode them anyway to quietly prove that he could), first-day-of-school feeling, and edge-of-cold-swimming-pool feeling—only much bigger, as though the swimming pool in front of him were several million miles deep.

"Proceed, Ambassador," said Protocol.

"Please be patient," said Gabe, still hesitating. "What am I supposed to do out there, exactly?"

The room made an exasperated noise. "I take it that your Envoy has not yet explained this to you. And I note that your world is without a registered Ambassador Academy. You have had no prior training. Splendid."

"You're making me feel less welcome," Gabe pointed out.

"I am very sorry," said Protocol, without contrition. "Experience trumps explanations, however, so I recommend that you simply proceed. Go meet your peers. Communicate as best you can, and try not to start an intergalactic incident. Have fun."

"Thanks," said Gabe. "Very helpful."

"You are most welcome," said Protocol. Gabe couldn't tell whether or not it was being sarcastic, but he very much suspected that it was. "Please proceed."

Gabe took a breath, let it out, and walked down the corridor. It was long, narrow, and made of the same thick and smoky glass stuff as the room behind it.

The corridor opened into a room big enough to have its own sky.

Clouds swirled and hovered in that sky. They looked more like the nebulae that Gabe had dreamed his way through than clouds of water vapor in the air back home.

Orange-tinted light came from every upward direction, as though local sunlight were setting everywhere at once.

The room itself looked like several landscapes squeezed into a gymnasium. Gabe saw things that looked like hills and trees, though shaped with simple, geometrical precision as though made rather than grown. And the colors were all unfamiliar, from purplish hillside plants to silvery tree leaves.

He saw caves set into the ground, a lake that looked more viscous than watery, and stranger features of the landscape that he wasn't even sure what to name. The Chancery looked alien to him. It also looked like a really big playground.

Kids were everywhere, climbing, running, swimming, building things together, or flying through layers of cloud. They all seemed human-shaped and Gabe-size, with hair and skin colors just a few shades different from what he was used to. This was disappointing. He had expected some green skin and tentacles.

Three of his fellow ambassadors seemed to be making sand castles out of the dark, blue-black sand of the lakeshore. Or maybe they were speaking to each other in some sort of sculpture-based language. Gabe watched from a distance, curious, but he couldn't really tell what they were doing.

He glanced away and accidentally caught sight of those same three ambassadors out of the corner of his eye.

They weren't human-shaped anymore.

One looked like a crab with the head of a camel.

Another looked like a lump of dandelion seeds.

The third was huge. That's all Gabe could tell at a glance. A face and one limb rested on the sand. The rest disappeared in the water.

Gabe stared at them directly. All three ambassadors looked human again: one crouching, one sitting, and one resting on his stomach with feet idly splashing the water behind him.

Gabe squinted. All three took on their very different shapes.

They only look like me when I look at them directly, he realized.

He squinted up at the flying ambassadors and caught glimpses of wings or waving tendrils. With eyes open wide he just saw kids, flying kids. They shouted and swooped, playing an airborne ball game.

The three on the beach might have been playing some sort of board game—but shaping the towers and tunnels of the board itself seemed at least as important as moving little stone pieces across it. He watched carefully, but he couldn't tell how to play, and he didn't feel comfortable intruding. He didn't feel comfortable at all. Instead he felt confused, disoriented, out of place—alien. Gabe didn't like this feeling, so he went walking and exploring to try to shake it off.

He couldn't shake it off, but the feeling shifted inside him. It traded awkwardness for awe.

We're not alone, he thought. He had always figured that aliens must exist somewhere. Space was entirely too big, filled with too many other stars and way too many other planets for the rest of it to stand empty. And he had known about the living reality of intelligent-yet-nonhuman life since his first chat with the Envoy. But the Envoy was just one purple oddity that fit in an aquarium. Now aliens *surrounded* Gabe. He squinted to glimpse the wide variety of shapes and movement. He was one of many. His own world was just one place among infinite many.

Gabe felt very small. He savored that feeling and kind of enjoyed it while he explored. Then he came to the forest. It looked like a coral reef and a massive jungle gym as much as it resembled terrestrial trees. Forest games apparently involved lots of running, hiding, and chasing. Gabe climbed a tree to get out of the way. The surface of the branches felt smoother than tree bark but not slippery.

He perched on a limb and watched the kids below. He

could recognize bits of hide-and-seek, tag, and capture the flag, but he wasn't sure how they fit together. There seemed to be teams, but players often switched sides.

Two other ambassadors climbed an adjacent tree. They both looked like girls, and both wore clothes similar to Gabe's. He resisted the sudden urge to squint at them, to find out what other shapes they might have. He felt like that would have been rude.

One stood upright on a thick branch. She had high cheekbones, a wide nose, and very straight, dark hair. She looked severe. Gabe thought that she should have pointy ears, but she didn't.

"Kaen," she said, and pointed to herself.

"Gabe," said Gabe. Then he hesitated, unsure what information they were supposed to swap. "Is Kaen your name or your species or where you're from? My name is Gabe. I'm from Earth. Or Terra. We call the planet Terra in Latin. That sounds more official somehow. Hi. I'm babbling. Sorry."

"Kaen," she said again. "I am the ambassador of the Kaen, which isn't my species, and it isn't my world. We don't have worlds. We are different species, all traveling in a great, nomadic fleet, and all together call ourselves the Kaen. Call me that. It isn't my name. I won't share my name with you."

"Fair enough," said Gabe. "Gabe is my name, but you're still welcome to use it."

"I will," she said, and stared at him. Gabe wondered if she was squinting, if she saw him now as he saw himself. He felt exposed and uncomfortable.

The other girl held on with both hands and both feet, crouching on her branch and mostly paying attention to the games below. She shrieked with laughter every time someone got tagged, and her laugh was much larger than herself.

"I'm Sapi," she said, without looking up. "My peer name is Sapi, anyway. Is hydrogen the most common element where you're from?"

"I'm Gabe," said Gabe. "And yeah, I think so."

"Good!" she said, delighted. "Everyone says so. If they know what I'm talking about. Hydrogen's everywhere." Sapi pulled a handful of leaves off the branch, wadded each one into a tight little ball, and threw them at the players on the ground. She laughed when they missed and she laughed when they hit. Some players shouted protests, but most of them just dodged.

Kaen was still staring at him. Gabe stood on his own branch and looked out over the Chancery, trying get a sense of the place and its size.

"Who made all this?" he asked.

Sapi looked up, surprised. "You don't have an academy, do you?"

Gabe felt a flush of embarrassment, along with a hefty helping of annoyance at the Envoy and Protocol for tossing him into a great big roomful of aliens without so much as a hint about what this would be like. He tried to shrug off the annoyance and shame.

"Nope," he said. "No academy. Just learning as I go."

"We all made it," said Kaen. "One piece at a time. We're still making it. Everybody's home environment helps to shape this one, so there should be one corner that feels like home to you. The rest is translated to look at least a little bit familiar."

She stood on her branch with her arms crossed, not moving. It looked kind of badass to stand in a tree without using her hands to hold on. Gabe wondered if she actually had hands, but he didn't squint at her to find out.

Sapi, by contrast, kept in constant motion. She jumped between branches, threw more wadded-up leaves, and tried to disrupt the games below.

"I didn't expect all this to be a big playground," Gabe said.

"Of course it is!" said Sapi. "*Everything* plays. And starting up a game is usually easier than talking."

"But we're ambassadors," Gabe protested. "Shouldn't

we be doing—I don't know—important diplomatic things?"

"You don't know very much about games, do you?" Kaen asked.

Gabe didn't know what to say to that.

"Be nice," said Sapi. "He's new and confused." She climbed from her branch to his and then leaned in close as though she had something extremely important and secret to say.

Gabe leaned in to listen. Sapi laughed when he did. "Have you noticed how different ambassadors have different comfort zones?"

That wasn't the sort of important secret Gabe had expected. "No," he said. "I haven't been here long enough to notice."

"It's hilarious," she told him in a whisper-laugh. "Some prefer to stand farther back and shout at each other, and others don't really consider it a conversation if their faces aren't touching. So when two ambassadors try to talk but don't agree on proper conversational distance, one of them is always moving in while the other is always moving back. They don't even notice it most of the time. It's like dancing. You'll see it happen if you stay up here in the trees long enough. Just look down and watch people talk." She reached over and tapped the tip of his nose.

"I'm glad you're not the sort who needs to be shouted at from a distance. Kaen over there doesn't mind close conversations, either—but only once she gets used to you, and that takes a while."

Kaen said nothing and did not move.

Gabe had noticed the same sort of thing living in Minneapolis. Lots of people there were Scandinavian, or at least descended from Scandinavians—tall, blond, and more accustomed to large conversational distances— whereas Gabe's family preferred nose-to-nose chats. So he felt perfectly fine an inch away from Sapi's face.

A part of Gabe *was* jumping up and down and shouting *Girl! Girl! Almost rubbing faces with someone girlish!* But he didn't have too much trouble ignoring that part. Sapi seemed like a girl to him, but he had no idea what she was like to herself. The inner voice shouting *Girl!* sounded far enough away.

"My turn for questions," he said. "I've got strange ships in my solar system. Not sure who they are. Not sure what they're doing, either. How do I find out?"

Kaen said nothing.

Sapi made a thoughtful, humming noise. "Who are your closest neighbors? Ask Protocol how to find them if you don't already know. Travel takes a while, so it's probably someone already nearby."

She jumped away and threw more leaves at the kids below.

Gabe plucked a leaf from his own branch. It felt more malleable than terrestrial tree leaves, more like a kind of sticky paper. He folded it into a leaf-paper airplane and then tossed it out and away from the forest.

Several other ambassadors broke away from their chasing game to watch it fly. They pulled down more foldable leaves to try making their own.

Gabe's flew farther than he thought it would. The plane sailed over hills and then whacked an ambassador in the back of the head.

The ambassador turned around. This one was tall and very pale, his skin whitish-blue. He stood apart from every game, but he didn't look like a newcomer. He looked like a predator. Everyone else seemed to avoid his company and move wide around him.

The pale ambassador noticed Gabe in the tree, and they shared one moment of eye contact.

Gabe waved. "Oops," he said. "Sorry!"

Another ball of leaves smacked the side of Gabe's face.

"Look away, look away, look away!" Sapi whispered. "Stupid! Don't talk to him. Don't even look at Omegan of the Outlast, not ever. Do you even have eyes? Most do, but not everybody. Light is a pretty efficient way to notice things, so practically everyone grows eyes. But sometimes they don't. If your species grew up in very deep caves, or down at the bottom of very deep oceans, or in the middle of very dense clouds, then maybe you didn't have enough light to bother with eyes. So you might not know what I'm talking about when I say, 'Don't look at him,' but try not to look at him anyway!"

"I've got eyes," said Gabe. He shot a quick look back at the pale and solitary ambassador. But that one no longer seemed to notice or care about Gabe's existence.

Sapi climbed up beside him. "Then stop challenging the Outlast by catching his attention! If his people come to your system, then you should run. Flee. Off you go, all of you, your whole species and whoever else you can bring along. You need to keep moving if you want to outlast them."

Gabe glared at her and wiped sticky leaf sap from his cheek. "Moving?"

"Yes, mooooooooooving," she said with exaggerated slowness as though speaking to an idiot. "Leaving the nest. Heading up and out to other worlds."

"We can't do that yet," Gabe admitted. "We *did* walk on the moon, though. I haven't been there, personally, but my people have."

"Your own moon?" Sapi asked.

"Yes . . . ," said Gabe.

"Well," she said, and leaped back to her own branch. "Well, well, well. That's tremendously impressive. Your own moon. Right there, big in your own sky. What a great place to run and hide. They'll *never* find you there. Forget about running, then. Just keep your head down. If you have one. Maybe you'll get to keep it."

Gabe plucked a leaf, wadded it up, and threw it at Sapi. It bounced off her forehead. She looked shocked for a moment and then laughed and laughed.

"You're worth talking to," she said, still laughing. "You might even be worth playing games with. Kaen, what do you think? Oh, she's gone already."

Gabe looked. Ambassador Kaen no longer stood on her branch, though Gabe hadn't noticed her leave.

"You seem to be leaving too," Sapi said. "Bye."

"What do you mean?" Gabe asked her. Then he felt a sudden, wrenching dizziness and woke up.

8

Gabe woke from his accidental nap at noon. The phone was ringing. He stumbled downstairs.

"Hello?" he said to the phone once he had found it. He wasn't fully awake yet. His only goal was to get the phone to stop ringing, and saying hello was how he got it to stop.

"Hello, my heart," said his mother. For one strange moment Gabe thought it was the Envoy on the phone. But the two of them didn't *really* sound the same, even though both used the same voice with the same accent. The rhythm was different. The Envoy's words were clipped, separate, and specific. Everything Mom said moved like water, flowing downstream from wherever it started to wherever it needed to be.

"Hi, Mom," said Gabe.

"I need you to do something for me," she said with a

hitch and a stumble in her voice—or maybe that was just crackling on the phone connection. "I need you to get a few diapers and wipes together. And pajamas for the twins. Toss all that in a bag."

"Okay," said Gabe. In his grogginess this sounded only slightly odd. "What's going on?"

"Frankie's mother is coming by to pick you up and bring you here," she told him, her voice careful and brittle.

Gabe became fully and completely awake at this news. He hadn't seen or spoken to Frankie's mom since the destruction of her backyard and everything in it, and he had been hoping to avoid her for as long as possible.

"What's going on?" he asked again. "Where are you?"

She told him.

The doorbell rang.

Frankie's mom was tall and always prickly cold. The two of them did not say much on the drive to the ICE detention center. This wasn't surprising. Frankie's mom never said much. ICE stood for "Immigration and Customs Enforcement," apparently. They drove to this icy place in a pocket of icy silence.

Gabe stared out the window. He wasn't sure he could speak if he tried. His brain and the rest of him seemed disentangled from each other.

The waiting room inside the detention center was a small place with a gray carpet, ten dingy-looking chairs, and a guard behind a counter. The guard was a woman who looked and sounded like old leather, the way serious cigarette smokers usually looked and sounded. She was polite enough. She didn't ask for Gabe's birth certificate, though he had brought it with him just in case he needed to prove where he was from.

Once the guard called his name, Gabe went through a large metal door that looked like it wasn't supposed to open, not ever. The door shut behind him with a sound that suggested it never would open again. *You are not welcome here,* the door said in its heaviness. *But now you can't leave.*

Gabe met his father in a small room. They sat down, facing each other, a thick glass barrier between them. Dad wore an orange jumpsuit and handcuffs on a long chain that connected to cuffs at his feet. He took very small steps to get to his chair.

"I brought the diapers," Gabe said first, and quickly, without saying hello. For some reason it seemed important to say that first and to say it in English. "I gave them to the guard in the waiting room."

His mouth and his brain still didn't feel connected. He tried to ask what happened, but he wasn't sure how.

Mom hadn't explained it all. Gabe wanted to know where she and Andrés and Noemi were, and why they weren't all right there, and he didn't know how to ask any of that either. He wanted to know if the twins were wearing tiny orange jumpsuits.

"I didn't stop at a stop sign," Dad said. He said it as though that were an adequate explanation. Gabe just blinked, because it wasn't really. "Not completely. I was sure that I did, but the officer said I didn't come to a *complete* stop."

"Okay," said Gabe. "That's something you can get arrested for?"

"No," said Dad. "But if you come to their attention, then they check your documents. And we don't have any. Your mother used to. She had a visa at first. But I don't. Never did."

He was trying to explain and trying to apologize and trying to understand himself how this had happened. Gabe knew that much, at least.

"We never meant to stay," Dad went on. "We figured we were nomads, your mother and I, and I always thought that by now we'd be in some other part of the world. But I had a friend who wanted to open up a restaurant here, so we came to help him out. We brought Lupe. And then we had you. Two kids kept us in one place for longer than we planned. Then we made the place home. I never thought we'd make a home somewhere with no defenses against howling arctic winds, you know? But we did. We stayed here."

He paused. Gabe nodded once to keep his father talking.

"They'll let your mother go soon," Dad went on. "Her and the twins. Tonight or maybe tomorrow morning. I don't know. But they'll *release her on recognizance*." He said the awkward, official words slowly. The syllables obviously tasted bitter to him. "They still *want* to deport her, but that'll take months to happen. More than a year, maybe. And she doesn't have to pay a bond now, luckily. They'll let the three of them go."

He said this in a reassuring way, or at least he tried to, but Gabe noticed immediately that his father hadn't said anything at all about himself.

"What about you?" Gabe asked. "When do they let you out?"

His father smiled with only half of his mouth, the way he did whenever the car broke, or when anything else broke, or when snowplows scraped the streets clean of a blizzard but blocked the driveway with a two-foot wall of solid ice and slush that the landlord was supposed to shovel but never actually did. It was Dad's *this sucks* expression.

"Me, they will throw out of the country. Immediately. Tomorrow morning." He paused to let that sink in. It didn't really sink in. Gabe just stared at him. He went on. "I don't get months of hearings and paperwork like your mother does because I've hopped the border before. I was a kid, first learning how to ride a motorcycle around the world. I got caught right away and sent home. So this is my second time getting deported, and there's no way to contest a second time. Not for ten years. In a decade I'll be allowed to ask permission for reentry, but not until then. Not even with four children on this side of the fence. And we can't all go south. They won't *let* us all go south. All this is going to take a long while to untangle, and we're going to rack up some mighty big phone bills between now and then. Maybe you can mow a few lawns this summer, earn extra cash to buy some long-distance phone time?"

Dad tried to maintain his half-smile, but he looked stricken. Whatever he felt right then, he was clearly trying hard not to feel it. His voice was half kidding, half serious, and entirely ashamed to tell Gabe that he would have to pitch in to pay for international phone bills.

Gabe needed to make that expression leave his father's face immediately, so he did the only thing he could think of. He leaned forward and spoke with the sort of earnest mock formality that Dad had used when he gave him a hammer of wisdom and truth.

"Every restaurant in this city will rise up in protest and demand your return," Gabe said in solemn promise.

Dad laughed, surprised. "Tell them not to give up hope," he answered. "Tell them that my spoon and saucepan will return to the kitchens of this city. Tell them to tighten their belts and be brave."

"I'll tell them," Gabe promised. "Somehow they'll endure other cooking while you're gone." Neither one of them joked about what Mom's cooking was usually like.

The leathery guard told them that time was up.

Dad's face got tense again. "Tell Lupe—something. Tell her I wish I could see her before I have to go. But I can't."

"She could still come visit you today," said Gabe, confused.

Dad gave him a warning look and dropped his voice. "Better not."

Gabe understood the warning, if not the reasons for it. He nodded. His father seemed to relax.

Gabe did not relax. His face hurt; all the muscles clenched with tension like they did whenever he and Frankie watched a horror movie.

I'm the ambassador of this entire world, Gabe thought.

All of it. But nobody here knows that. I can talk to aliens thousands of light-years away, but we'll need to scramble for cash so I can keep talking to Dad by phone.

He said good-bye to his father through the glass barrier.

On the way home Gabe began to unfreeze and unclench. He tried not to. He wasn't sure what would happen if he let himself feel the way he actually felt.

9

Frankie's mother actually spoke on the drive back. "Your sister Guadalupe is at my house already. You should all stay there for dinner and then stay the night. There's also a Pack 'n Play for the twins to sleep in. I'm sorry that Frankie isn't home. He'll be in California for the rest of the summer."

"I know," said Gabe. "He told me."

Her voice was still sharp, like ice sculptures carved with chain saws, but it seemed to have emotion in it somewhere. She really did sound sorry.

"Can you drop me off at home first?" he asked. "I need to feed the pets before coming over."

"Of course," said Frankie's mom. She pulled up in front of Gabe's house. "I'll see you at dinner. I have to go back to work for the rest of the afternoon, but hurry over as soon as you can. Hopefully your mother and the toddlers will be out before dinner, and your mother will need the help. I understand that the little ones listen to you more than they listen to Guadalupe."

She made a point of pronouncing Lupe's full name with a Spanish accent, which made it leap out and away from everything else that she said.

"The twins don't listen to anyone," said Gabe, "but I'll hurry. Thank you for the ride. And for everything."

"This was the plan," she told him. "Taking refuge at our house has always been part of your emergency plans. See you at dinner."

The car drove away. Gabe went inside.

In the kitchen, on the card table that Gabe's father used as extra counter space, Gabe found the cane sword, the vajra hammer, and a Post-it note from Lupe.

Emergency Plan #23, read the note.

"Isn't number twenty-three the one about ghost pirates?" he said to himself. "Or else disappearing family members. That would make more sense." She probably wrote it to let him know she was over at Frankie's house, but he knew that already.

He fixed himself some cereal as a late lunch. This was a sorry meal after the greasy magnificence of his breakfast— the last meal his father had cooked in this kitchen before leaving to run errands, get arrested, and get deported.

Gabe shut the door on that thought and finished his cereal.

He heard the plaintive scratching noises of unhappy pets and brought food dishes up to his room. All three pets expressed their unhappiness to him when he got there. Garuda's complaints were the most subtle. He stood and stared with silent reproach. The fox and the bird were both louder.

"Sorry, everyone," said Gabe. He checked his closet for the Envoy and found only an empty aquarium. "The Envoy isn't here, which means that it's probably in the basement, which means that the basement might still be filled with hazardous physics. So you all have to stay here."

Sir Toby tried to make a break for it anyway when Gabe left the room. Gabe gently nudged the fox back with his toe and shut the door. He hated keeping them confined. He hated the whole idea of confinement.

Gabe went all the way downstairs to find the Envoy.

The wire frame in the basement had grown larger and more complicated since that morning. Red sparks constantly exploded from it, and most of those sparks joined a spiraling vortex of dust motes that fell through the dryer's open door and disappeared there.

The Envoy scooted around the whole mess, working furiously.

"Not done yet?" Gabe asked, stating the obvious.

The Envoy made a mouth.

"No," it said. "Not done. And I don't understand the problem! The black hole should have completely dissipated by now. It should have ejected all the substance it had absorbed already—except for your entangled particles, because we sent those elsewhere. But it hasn't collapsed. It won't collapse. Nothing I do will make it collapse. It's as though something is working against me, deliberately keeping this open. I don't like that idea."

Gabe didn't like that idea either. "How dangerous is it?"

"I have it contained to the clothes dryer," the Envoy said. "The rest of the house should be safe."

This wasn't actually an answer. "Should be?" Gabe pressed.

"Should be," said the Envoy. It scooted quickly back and forth. Red sparks flew.

Gabe sat on the steps to watch warily. "My parents are getting deported," he said, his voice flat and gray in his own ears.

The Envoy stopped working, clearly unsure how to respond. "I'm so very sorry!" it said. "Sympathies. Condolences. This is terrible."

"I also dreamed about the Embassy this morning," Gabe went on, his voice still flat and gray.

"That part is good news," the Envoy said cautiously. "Though I'm sorry that I've been unable to prepare you for your arrival in advance. Protocol does get testy about that."

"I noticed," said Gabe.

The conversation ended when red sparks burst from every joint of the wire frame at once.

The Envoy sputtered something in a different language and a different voice. It sounded like creative cursing.

"We'll have to talk later," it said, using Mom's voice again. "I should focus on my struggle with this appliance to keep it from killing us."

Gabe climbed down from the staircase and carefully approached to get a closer look at the misbehaving contraption. Then everything went wrong.

The dryer imploded. The frame around it collapsed. Sparks appeared and disappeared again, just as quickly.

The Envoy scrambled away from the chaotic mess. It shouted something, but Gabe couldn't hear through the sudden rush of air. The Envoy's mouth reached out like a hand. Gabe took it, and the two of them raced up the basement stairs while the basement behind them ceased to exist.

Gabe realized that the pets were all upstairs, trapped

in his bedroom. Every single one of Dad's emergency plans demanded a quick exit in case of fire or poltergeist or any other circumstance in which the house itself had become dangerous. They didn't have an emergency plan for black holes in the basement, but the principle was the same: Get out. Get out now. Let firefighters fight their way into the burning house to rescue pets. Let exorcists fight their way into a haunted house. Get out.

Gabe hated that rule. He still followed it.

The Envoy tugged him toward the kitchen door. Gabe let go of its hand-mouth to grab both cane sword and vajra hammer from the table. That was not part of the emergency plan, but they were right there, and grabbing them didn't slow him down. Then he grabbed his jump bag from the coat hook on the way out. That *was* part of the plan. He noticed that Lupe's bag was already gone.

Gabe and the Envoy made it as far as a tree in the very back of the backyard, beside the fence. The boy braced himself against the far side of that tree. The Envoy wrapped itself around the trunk. Behind them the foundation and first floor of the duplex collapsed in on itself. It did so silently. Air that would have carried sound was sucked into the vortex along with the house. Gabe heard nothing but wind, howling and furious, rushing into the yard to fill up the suddenly empty space.

The vortex compressed, collapsed, and vanished. The top half of the house fell into the hole where the rest of it used to be. Gabe felt the impact through his feet and legs more than he heard it happen.

The wind subsided. Gabe came out from behind the tree trunk, breathing hard, grateful that the air around him held still long enough to be breathable.

The second floor of his house stuck up from a hole in the ground. Gabe could see his bedroom window. He saw Zora tap her beak against the glass. He dropped the jump bag, ran across the yard, and yanked open the window sash to rescue his pets.

Zora hopped onto his head and clung there with her claws. She made several chirrupy noises of alarm.

Garuda sat on the bookshelf near the window. The shelf still stood, though all the books had fallen out. The lizard looked intrigued by recent events, but not especially alarmed. Gabe caught him up and held him. Then he called for Sir Toby. He couldn't see the fox, but the bedroom door was still shut so he had to be in there somewhere.

It felt bizarre to peer into his second-floor bedroom while standing on the ground, as though he had suddenly grown very tall. He stuck his head farther inside, and smelled smoke. "Of course," he said. "Of *course* there's smoke."

"I also smell smoke," said the Envoy beside him. "Broken wiring may have ignited insulation in the walls. The insulation is very old and made out of flammable paper. Not at all sensible. I noticed that hazard while crawling between walls yesterday."

"Sir Toby is still in my room." Gabe wanted to go back in. He wasn't supposed to go back in. It was expressly against the emergency plan to go back inside. He almost went in anyway.

"Stop," the Envoy insisted. "I'm less fragile than you." It climbed through the window like a slinky in reverse, found the fox underneath Gabe's bed, and herded him out from under the blankets. Sir Toby yip-barked, angry at being herded. Then the fox saw Gabe through the open window and made a running jump in his direction.

Gabe caught Sir Toby, tucked him under his other arm, and backed away from the wreckage. The Envoy oozed out and followed him.

Thick, dark smoke began to billow through every open window. They stood by the tree and watched the house burn. Zora chirped from the top of Gabe's head.

"The kitchen is gone," Gabe whispered. "Dad's spice rack is gone. He's really proud of that spice collection."

"I'm very sorry for the loss," said the Envoy.

"What just happened, exactly?" Gabe asked, still too astonished to be upset. "How did this happen?"

"The disaster triggered when you approached the clothes dryer," said the Envoy. It shifted colors from pale purple to dark indigo-blue, like the sky when the sun is almost entirely gone. Its voice was cold, colder than Gabe had ever heard his mother's voice before. "Someone just tried to kill you, Ambassador. Someone tried to *assassinate* you. And they knew enough about the entanglement process to sabotage it. Only one of your own colleagues could have done this. And they might already know that they have not succeeded. We need to get you away from this place."

Sirens wailed in the distance, growing louder.

Gabe hoisted up the backpack and pets. He tucked the vajra hammer through a belt loop and the cane sword under one arm. Zora remained perched on his head.

"Follow me," he said, and set out for Frankie's house.

10

Gabe cut through alleyways and the rocket-scorched lawn of Frankie's backyard. He found the spare key under the fake rock in the garden and let himself in through the kitchen door. The Envoy followed behind him.

The kitchen looked shiny and new—or at least parts of it did, like the stainless steel fridge and the glass tiles on the wall behind the counter. It was much bigger than the one at Gabe's place—the one that *used to be* at his place, when it still existed, which was just fifteen minutes ago. That kitchen must be even smaller now, compressed to a tiny point of condensed mass. Or else maybe it was *bigger* now, its molecules expelled from the collapse of the black hole and scattered to the winds, covering the whole city. Either way, it was gone.

Gabe dropped his backpack, put the fox and the iguana on the floor, set the hammer and cane on the kitchen table beside a pile of textbooks, and then closed all the doors to keep the pets from escaping the kitchen. Zora made a flying circuit of the room and then perched back on the top of Gabe's head. Fox and iguana claws made clackety clackety noises against the floor tiles while they explored.

Gabe sat down on a kitchen chair, hard. He couldn't think straight. His head was spinning, and the centrifugal force flung coherent thought out his ears.

The Envoy tapped Gabe's knee. "We should probably keep moving," it said, gentle but insistent.

"Where?" asked Gabe. Emergency plans ended here. *If home burns, grab your jump bag and get to Frankie's house.* Home had burned. The top half of it did, anyway. And now Gabe had made it to Frankie's house.

"I don't know where," said the Envoy. "But there's a chance that our attackers can track the energy signature of your newly entangled particles and find us here."

"That's bad," said Gabe.

"Yes," the Envoy agreed.

"So what happens if they find us?" Gabe asked. "Can they send other small black holes after us?"

"No. Your entanglement is complete. But I don't know what else they might do. And they must be nearby, closer even than the ships in the asteroid belt. We should be moving. We should make it more difficult for them to find you."

Gabe didn't move. He didn't feel like he could. He needed to keep sitting down. He also needed a drink of water. The pets were heavy, and he'd run all the way there. He was supposed to *stay there*. The plans said so. Dad said so. Frankie's mother had said so.

"Give me a sec to think about this," he said, or at least started to say.

Footsteps thudded against stairs. *That must be Lupe*, Gabe thought. *Frankie's mom doesn't make any noise when she moves through the house. Frankie's mom is more like a ninja than a pirate.*

He expected his sister to burst into the kitchen the way she usually burst into a room, but he didn't expect her to do it through a secret door in the kitchen wall. One of the wooden panels swung open, and his sister thundered through.

"Mom?" she called. "I thought I heard Mom . . ."

The Envoy scootched under the table and out of sight.

"Mom's not here," said Gabe. "She's in jail. No, not jail. A detention center. They'll let her out soon. But not Dad. Why didn't you come? Why are you hiding out in a secret room? *And how is there a secret room in Frankie's house?* He can't keep any secrets, not to save his own life or anyone else's. He would have told me about a secret room!"

Gabe didn't think anything could surprise him. Several unexpected and unsettling things had happened today already. But he didn't know how to handle the existence of secret doors and hidden staircases in his best friend's kitchen. This was like finding out that his sister was Zorro *and* Batman, both of them at once, and always had been.

"That's *why* Frankie doesn't know," Lupe told him. "This isn't a playroom. This is history. Frankie's mom didn't want him to wreck the place or break the door. And he probably would have."

Gabe admitted that Frankie probably would have broken the door.

"And I didn't go with you to the detention center because I would have been detained, dumbass." She shook her head. "Mom and Dad never wanted to worry your poor, innocent little brain, but it's absolutely stupid that we've never talked about this. We made plans for it, along with all of Dad's ridiculous poltergeist plans, but we've never just talked about it. Not with you."

Dots connected inside Gabe's innocent brain. He resented the word *dumbass*, but he swallowed that resentment and let himself begin to understand.

"You weren't born here," he said. Lupe had been tiny when Mom and Dad moved north. Gabe knew that already, but he hadn't ever thought about it. It was just one of the many ways he considered his sister more interesting than himself. She had a more concrete connection to family history than he did. She was actually from the legendary city of their parents, a place Gabe himself had never been.

"Nope," she said. "I wasn't. I don't remember living anywhere else, but I'm not actually from here. You are. That makes all the difference. That's why I'm hiding." She said it like this was his fault. Then she saw the look on his face and softened her own. "How are they?"

"I only saw Dad," said Gabe. He relayed their conversation, almost word for word, while trying not to think much about any of those words. They sat in silence when he was done.

Sir Toby tried to climb through the secret door. Lupe stopped him with her toe.

"Go take a peek," she said, gesturing up the tiny spiral stairs.

Gabe took Zora off his head, set her on the table, and went up.

The stairs were rough, without paint or lacquer, like stairs going down to an unfinished basement. They creaked under Gabe's feet as he cautiously climbed. At the top he found a room. It was small. The whitewashed plaster walls were oddly shaped, as though otherwise unused corners of the house had been stuck together and tucked away. There were no windows. A small bed took up most of the space.

Gabe crept back down the narrow stairs. He gave Lupe a look filled with large question marks.

"Underground Railroad stop," she explained. "The chimney still has a mark advertising this as a safe house. Most of the railroad ran east of the Great Lakes, but a few lines still came through here. A lot of people who weren't slaves anymore slept in that room. Frankie's family used it again to help refugees from El Salvador and Honduras. Canada offered asylum, but the US usually didn't, so they needed to sneak their way north. Frankie's mom used to help drive that route in the eighties when she was barely older than I am. She doesn't do that much anymore, but she still takes people in. Remember Sophia?"

Gabe did, but only barely. "Exchange student," he said. "Lived here for a bit. Used to babysit me and Frankie. You were friends, right?"

"She wasn't an exchange student," said Lupe. "She left Honduras and walked here by herself. She passed dried-up bodies in the Arizona desert—people who died of thirst or were shot by rednecks and dumped by the roadside. She stayed here when she got this far. Sophia told me what she was running from. She told me what happened to her brothers. But I'm not going to tell you any of it."

She shut the wall panel. It looked ordinary now. Gabe found it odd that the secret place sat so comfortably next to shiny new kitchen appliances. History hadn't ended. It wasn't over. It just overlapped with now.

Lupe held out her hand to Zora.

"Meow!" said the bird. She pooped on the table and then hopped onto the outstretched hand. Lupe stroked the feathers of her neck. Gabe fetched a paper towel to clean the poop.

"Wait a sec," said Lupe. "Why did you bring all the pets with you? You should have left them at the house."

"The house burned down," Gabe told her.

"What?"

"It burned down."

"I heard you, but *what*? What did you do? Did you pick the worst possible day to build another stupid rocket?"

A black hole ate it, Gabe thought. *Aliens tried to assassinate me with physics.*

"I don't know how it happened," he said aloud. "But I saved your sword. And the pets."

"Stupid!" she yelled at him. "Save yourself first. Leave the pets for the firefighters. That's the plan, remember? We just went through all the plans this morning!"

Gabe ignored the insult and said nothing.

Lupe took up the hammer of wisdom and truth as if she wanted to find more spiders—or as if she suddenly considered Gabe to be a spider. She whacked the pile of textbooks on the table.

"Are those from summer school?" Gabe asked, hoping to deflect attention away from himself.

"Yes," she said. "I went to class this morning. Mother will be so very proud."

Gabe watched her quietly boil. He connected more dots. "What happened last year? Why did you start failing classes all of a sudden?"

Lupe glared at him. "That doesn't matter."

"What happened?" Gabe asked again, his voice low and relentless.

"That absolutely does not matter," she insisted. "We've got worse to worry about than my academic record."

Much worse, Gabe silently agreed, but he took the hammer of wisdom and truth away from his sister and waved it at her. "Tell me."

She took back the hammer and gave the books a few more frustrated whacks.

"Last year I met with Mr. Paul Arpaio, the career counselor at school," she told him. She said the name with exaggerated, sarcastic formality and antirespect. "That's it. That's the only thing that happened. I was working on my college applications. He told me not to bother. He told me that he controlled all the transcript files, that no college would ever see mine. And he told me to start walking south."

Gabe felt the spark-bright beginnings of rage building in him. He wasn't really sure what to do about it. Dad and Lupe were the ones with quick tempers. They knew how to boil over, how to explode and still be whole afterward. Gabe didn't know how to do that. He tried to ignore the rage-sparks inside him. He hoped they would just go away.

"He was supposed to help you get *into* college," Gabe said, "not keep you *out*."

"Yeah, well, he's helping *citizens* get in by making sure *aliens* with perfect grades can't. Not that I have perfect grades anymore."

"I'm pretty sure that's illegal," said Gabe. "It has to be."

Lupe laughed her bitter laugh. "*I'm* illegal, you idiot."

Gabe ignored both insults—the one aimed at him, and the one she had shot back at herself. It took effort to ignore them. "Did you tell Mom?"

"No. And neither will you. It would break her heart

and then kick all the broken pieces around afterward. I let her think my grades slipped over a boy. Dad suspects otherwise, but he hasn't asked me for details. So anyway, summer school doesn't matter. Not in any way does it matter. Improving my transcript won't matter, because no college will ever see it—and also because Mom and Dad are getting deported. And because our house burned down. I can't believe it burned down *today*. You get to tell Mom. I'm not going to."

I shouldn't be here to tell her, Gabe thought. *I need to get away from all of you. Someone might blow another hole in the world wherever I happen to be.* But he wasn't sure how to leave, exactly. They had lost too much today already. The house was gone. Dad was in an orange jumpsuit and took very small steps with his feet chained together. Mom would need Gabe to look after the twins most of the time. He couldn't just leave. But he couldn't stay, either. Alien assassins might attack at any moment and hurt anyone who happened to be standing nearby.

This would be difficult to explain.

He was still trying to figure out how to tell Lupe that he had to run away when she accidentally kicked the Envoy under the table. It rolled across the floor, cleared its throat, and tried to recover its dignity.

Lupe stood up. She began to hiccup. She tried to stop. Gabe got her a glass of water.

Oh well, he thought. *Guess I won't be keeping this part a secret.*

"Lupe, this is the Envoy," he said. "Envoy, this is my sister."

The Envoy ducked its mouth in a sort of bow. "Honored," it said. "Charmed. Hello. Hi, there. Greetings to you. I've heard that gargling can sometimes cure the hiccups."

Lupe held the glass of water as if she didn't remember what glasses of water were for. "What is that thing?" she whispered. "It sounds like Mom."

"Yes," said the Envoy. "I've mimicked the shape of her vocal cords to sound comforting and familiar."

Lupe sat down, sipped her water, and continued to hiccup while Gabe and the Envoy took turns explaining that her little brother Gabriel Sandro Fuentes had become the Ambassador of Terra and all Terran life. Neither one of them mentioned the assassination attempt. Gabe just told her "something went wrong" with the basement entanglement—something that needed fixing, somewhere else, somewhere not here. He wasn't very good at lying. He was far better at keeping quiet, keeping secrets hidden, than he was at lying about them. Lupe noticed, of course.

"Well, that's extremely vague," she said. "I can't let you wander off alone! Not ever. *Definitely* not today. We need to stay here and wait for Mom."

"I'm not alone," said Gabe. "The Envoy's an adult."

Lupe took up the hammer of wisdom and truth. She walked around the table, bent down, and whacked the Envoy with it.

"Hey!" Gabe cried out.

"Ouch," said the Envoy.

"Just checking to see if it's an illusion I can smash," said Lupe without apology. She sat down again. "I hate that it uses Mom's voice. *I absolutely hate that.* But at least I feel a little bit less like an alien now that I've met one."

"I'm not technically alien to this world," the Envoy said, but Lupe ignored it. She hiccuped and gargled the last of her water. Then she stared at Gabe for a long, unsettling amount of time.

"You'll be good at this ambassador thing," she decided.

"You keep calling me an idiot," Gabe pointed out.

"I said you *will* be good at this, not that you already are. But you learn fast. Just don't blow up the world like you blew up our house."

"The house didn't explode," the Envoy explained. "It *imploded.* It blew down rather than blowing up, and only caught fire afterward."

Lupe didn't respond or even look at the Envoy. She clearly felt uncomfortable about the existence of the Envoy. *Maybe she's too old already,* Gabe thought. *She's smart. She's curious. She makes new friends easily. But maybe she isn't quite neotenous enough.*

"We should go, Ambassador," the Envoy said, quietly insistent.

Gabe stood up to go. She wouldn't let him leave if she thought he was in serious danger—but the serious danger was why he had to go. He didn't think he could explain, so he just had to leave.

"You can trust the Envoy to look after me," he said.

In that moment he realized that *he* trusted the Envoy.

Lupe glared at him as if she were trying to set him on fire with her mind. Then she dug in her pocket and gave him all her spare cash.

"Buy a cheap, disposable cell phone and text me the number," she told him. "That's the only way I'm letting you out of my sight. And move your ass, strawberry. Hurry up with whatever important ambassador business you've got going. I don't even want to think about trying to explain this to Mom when she gets here, so you need to get back first. The twins listen to you more than me. You really need to be here."

"Okay," said Gabe.

Sure, he said to himself. *I'll do my best to deal with a potentially deadly intergalactic incident by dinnertime. Wish me luck.*

He opened the backpack, invited the Envoy to climb inside, and hoisted the heavy thing over his shoulder.

"Take the cane," Lupe said.

Gabe just blinked at her. "Dad gave that to you. You're the oldest. You're the fighter. It's yours."

"Take it," she said again. "I still expect you to bring it back."

Gabe took his great-grandfather's walking cane. It did make him feel better to carry it, to have mighty secrets and hidden Toledo steel.

Lupe reached out with the mallet of wisdom and truth. Gabe gave it a fist bump. The beads rattled. Then he left the house through the kitchen door.

He paused in the middle of Frankie's backyard and wondered where he should go.

Away, he thought. *Just keep moving.*

He took a few steps. Then he turned around for one last look at his emergency refuge, the only safe place that he knew.

An energy beam burned through the sky and scorched the spot where he had been standing.

PART THREE
ATTACKED

11

Gabe ran until he couldn't. Then he half-walked, half-jogged. His scalp itched while he waited for another energy beam to incinerate him.

It didn't happen. Maybe the assassins weren't in geo-synchronous orbit and had to swing back around the world before taking another shot. Maybe.

His breath caught up with him. He noticed which direction he was going and decided it was a good direction. Then he ducked into a corner store to buy a cheap, disposable cell phone.

The building had four stories. Four ceilings stood between him and the sky, between him and whatever hostile thing was shooting at him from the other side of the sky.

He paced the store, waiting for another blast that didn't come.

He stood still, waiting. It still didn't come.

The front door of the corner store made an obnoxious, electronic beep when someone opened it. Gabe jumped. His heart smacked against the inside of his rib cage.

Someone is shooting at me. They imploded my house. They destroyed Dad's kitchen. Dad is getting kicked out of the country. Lupe is getting kicked out of college before she even gets to go.

Gabe's new rage-sparks blazed. More of him caught on fire. He didn't know how to handle that. He didn't know what to do about it.

Then he thought of something that he could do.

The store clerk obviously assumed that Gabe was an inept and fidgety shoplifter plagued by preemptive guilt, and kept a suspicious eye on him.

"Can I help you?" the clerk asked in a way that meant *I doubt it, and I'd rather not.*

"I need a phone," said Gabe. The cell phones on the counter in front of him were much too fancy to buy with Lupe's cash. Each was a pocket-size computer screen. "Can I see one that plays videos?" he asked, pointing.

A quick search found what he was looking for online: last year's commencement speech at Lupe's school, which had been taped by the phone cameras of proud parents.

"Hello, everyone," said the little screen in a friendly, folksy voice. "I'm Principal Ginny Brewer. Welcome, friends and family of the graduating seniors of Southeast High!"

The clerk stepped back to let Gabe play with a phone that he obviously wasn't going to actually buy. It was chained to the counter, so Gabe couldn't steal it without bolt cutters. The clerk still watched him, just in case he had bolt cutters.

Gabe set his backpack on the counter, next to the phone. "Listen to this," he whispered to the backpack. The Envoy made an impatient noise, but couldn't extend its throat enough to actually answer.

After watching Principal Brewer's speech, Gabe did another quick Internet search and found the phone number he needed. Then he dug Lupe's wad of cash out of his pocket and purchased a cheaper, disposable phone.

The corner store wasn't far from a light-rail train stop, and the train would be the quickest way to become a moving target. He hurried to the stop. He paced while waiting. He tried not to look up. The top of his scalp still itched in anticipation of shots fired from orbit.

The train arrived. Gabe hopped on board and hoped it was fast enough to keep alien weapons from getting a fix on his location. In his head he apologized to everyone else on the train for putting them in danger just by riding with them, just by sitting nearby.

If his attackers were in orbit, then they might be on the far side of the world at that moment. Or they might have already circled the globe and come back again, ready for another shot. Or else they might still be directly above him, moving as the world moved, taking careful aim. Gabe didn't know. He didn't have any idea how much time would pass before they tried again. He didn't even know who they were. The vast expanse of everything he did not know stretched away from him in every direction. He felt like he was drowning in ignorance.

But he did have one thing that he planned to do with the low, slow rage simmering inside him.

He thought about taking the train as far as the Mall of America, which was huge and easy enough to hide in. But the great big mall was always crowded, and he didn't want to endanger more bystanders. He needed to find a place with fewer people nearby.

After that he needed to figure out why he was under attack at all.

Gabe disembarked at Minnehaha Falls, a large stretch of urban park. He was supposed to come here anyway for the summer reading project—though writing an essay about Hiawatha didn't seem too important now. But he could still hide there. He could be alone there. He raced into the park as quickly as he could with a heavy, Envoy-filled bag on his back.

Minnehaha was supposed to mean "laughing water" in Dakota, but it didn't. It just meant "waterfall." So *Minnehaha Falls* was actually redundant, like saying "waterfall falls."

Gabe followed sidewalk trails. He passed a statue of Hiawatha and Minnehaha. He kept looking up. Bright and fluffy clouds crossed the blue sky and gave no hint of what might be searching for him on the other side.

His stomach complained. He glanced up again and realized that it was early evening already. He needed to eat something.

He bought fish tacos from the park restaurant. It was the cheapest thing on the menu. He crossed his fingers and hoped that alien assassins did not attack while he stood in line. He kept glancing at the ceiling, expecting it to burn.

"Hungry?" he whispered to his backpack. The Envoy still didn't have enough room to make a mouth and throat for itself, so its answer sounded more like a whispered burp than a word.

"I didn't catch that," Gabe whispered. "Do it again, once for yes and twice for no. Are you hungry?"

The backpack burped twice, so Gabe ordered food just for himself. Once he had his tacos, he went back outside and struck out across the park, keeping away from joggers, picnics, and people with strollers. He ate while he walked. The food vanished before he really noticed it was there. It must have been good.

The last time he had come here he'd chased the twins around for hours. He couldn't help looking around for them now, constantly noticing their absence, constantly reminding himself that they were not here with him—and that he wouldn't be at the Underground Railroad stop that was also Frankie's house when the twins arrived. They would need him, but Gabe and Dad would both be gone.

He forced himself to think practical thoughts. *I should find cover. Something thick and substantial to hide under.* He hurried down a long staircase to the bottom of the falls. The staircase ended at a stone and cement bridge that crossed the creek and led to a hiking trail.

Gabe looked around. He didn't see anyone else there, hiking or posing for pictures in front of the waterfall. He jumped the railing, scrambled down the rocky slope, and ducked underneath the bridge. Several boulders poked up from the creek. Gabe climbed onto one of them. The stone surface was cold, sheltered from sunlight. Gabe sat over the water and under cement, which seemed thick, solid, and possibly safe from orbital energy beams.

He opened his backpack and let the Envoy out.

"Why are we hiding under a bridge?" it asked.

"Because someone's shooting at us," said Gabe. "From orbit. They tried once in Frankie's backyard, but they missed."

"I wondered what that noise was," said the Envoy. It stretched out and poked the cement above them. "This might provide adequate shelter for now. You should take the opportunity to sleep."

Gabe just laughed. "You think I should sleep while perched on a cold rock and hiding from death rays?"

"Yes," the Envoy insisted. "To survive, you must learn who is trying to kill you. To serve your world as ambassador, you must learn who is trying to sever diplomatic contact and why. It's most likely whoever is in those ships among the asteroids. You'll have to go back to the Embassy to learn these things. And to go back to the Embassy you have to be asleep. Entangled travel will get easier as you get used to it—you'll be able to slip into a trance whenever you need to and then return at will. Eventually. But you don't have that skill yet, so just try to sleep instead."

"Right," said Gabe. "Sure. I'll try to sleep. But first I

need your help with something. I need your voice. I need you to copy someone else's."

The rage in Gabe glowed, desperate for something to do.

Only one Paul Arpaio lived in southeast Minneapolis, and his home phone number had been easy to find.

"Hello, Paul," said the Envoy in Principal Brewer's folksy voice. "You're fired, I'm afraid."

Gabe held the phone to the Envoy's puppetish mouth. He heard shocked sputtering on the other side of the conversation.

"I have complaints from the parents of *several* students you've threatened, Paul."

Lupe couldn't be the only one. Gabe was sure of that. If the counselor savored his power over students so much, then he wouldn't be content to savor it only once. And pretending that several students had come forward to complain should keep this from coming back around to Lupe.

He heard Mr. Arpaio continue to sputter.

"Now please don't make a stink about this," the Envoy interrupted. "I'm not going to report you, but don't expect a reference. Come clean out your desk first thing tomorrow. Yes, even though it's summer. I want this to be quick and painless. Good-bye, Paul."

Gabe hung up the phone. He felt a kind of satisfaction he had never experienced before. He usually tried to make conflicts vanish, to keep everyone else as happy as possible. This new feeling was a different, brooding sort. This was how Batman must feel after punching someone who needed to be punched. "Perfect," he said. "Thank you, Envoy."

The Envoy changed the shape of its throat to use Gabe's mother's voice. "You are welcome, Ambassador. I hope it works."

"Me too," said Gabe. "The guy sounded scared and pissed, right?"

"He did," the Envoy confirmed. "Very agitated. Very angry. And also frightened."

"Then he'll either keep his head down and go away quietly, or he'll go shouting. He might want to make someone else feel as small and helpless as he does right now, so he won't have to feel that way anymore. Maybe he'll say horrible things to other people in the office on his way out."

The Envoy nodded its mouth. "So if he burns his ships and bridges tomorrow morning, then he won't be able to go back to his old job regardless—even though he hasn't actually been fired."

"That's the idea," said Gabe.

"Is this how you feel as well, Ambassador?" the Envoy asked. "Did you need to make someone else feel as small and helpless as you do?"

Gabe didn't answer that.

He sent a text to Lupe instead.

Here's my new phone number.

She sent an answering text quickly. Got it.

And you should keep going to summer school, Gabe went on. It took a while for him to type out each letter. He'd never owned a phone before, and his thumbs weren't used to typing with it. Your college counselor just got fired.

?!??!?!?!?!?!?!!, she replied.

It's true, Gabe typed. Gotta go now. Bye.

His new phone rang as Lupe tried to actually call him. Gabe made it stop ringing by pushing buttons at random, and then he stuck the phone in his backpack.

"Okay," he said. "That's done. Now how do I search for assassins? What should I do, wander around the Chancery at random and shout, 'Hey, anybody here trying to kill me?'"

The Envoy sighed. It sounded so much like Mom's exasperated sigh that Gabe felt something fracture inside him.

"No, you probably shouldn't do that," said the Envoy.

"I'm sure you'll be able to figure out a more subtle way to investigate. Ask Protocol for help—even though Protocol will be reluctant to give it. You might try—"

Gabe interrupted. He couldn't pay attention to what it was saying, not at all—not when it used that voice to say it with. "Stop talking," he said. "Stop talking like her. It isn't comforting. You need to sound like someone else."

The Envoy paused. Then it reorganized its mouth and throat.

"Is this more comfortable for you to hear?" it asked in a deeper, more concerned, and completely unfamiliar voice. "Are you more at ease now?"

Gabe shook his head. "No. Not really. Never mind. I guess I'm used to her voice coming out of your mouth, so it's actually worse to hear you sound like a stranger. I'm sorry. Go back to using hers."

The Envoy reshaped its vocal cords again. It spoke kindly and cautiously with Gabe's mother's voice. "How's this?"

"Better," said Gabe. "Thank you." He curled up on the cold stone. "Keep watch while I nap, okay? Wake me up if we're under attack."

"I'll keep watch," the Envoy promised. "Sleep well. Learn as much as you can. Then act on the best information you have while also doubting what you think you know."

"Right," Gabe said. "That sounds easy."

"Nothing worth doing is easy, Ambassador."

Gabe tried to sleep.

He tried not to think about the word *deportation*.

He thought about the *Hiawatha* poem instead, the one he was supposed to read this summer, the one that called this place "Laughing Water." Remembering the poem shaped his thoughts into that same plodding rhythm, like a tune stuck in his head. He put his own words to the rhythm.

> *Now Ambassador Fuentes*
> *fled the burning of his household,*
> *fled the death rays from the heavens*
> *and took refuge in the parkland*
> *by the falls that were not laughing.*

The sound of the flowing creek and the *THUMP thump THUMP thump* of the words in his head calmed him down and slowed his pulse.

He slept.

"Ambassador Gabriel Sandro Fuentes, be welcome."

12

"Hi, Protocol," said Gabe.

"Hello, Ambassador. Is this self-image to your liking?"

Gabe looked in the mirror. "Looks great," he said, though he wasn't really sure about the ears.

"Excellent." Protocol almost sounded pleased. The mirror-door slid open. "Proceed."

Gabe did not proceed. "I'm going to need some help," he told the room around him.

"Very well," said Protocol. It sounded weary again. "How may I assist you?"

Gabe wasn't even sure which questions to ask. He didn't know how much he didn't know. "I'm . . . not sure who to talk to out there."

"Your Envoy still has not explained very much to you, I take it." The room made large and impatient noises. "Very well. It is obviously not possible for anyone to perceive the full size of this place at any one time, no matter how many eyes you happen to have or how impressive your cognitive ability. It is vast. It contains far too many entangled occupants. Both the place itself and the ambassadors gathered inside it are filtered down. You cannot see most of the Chancery while inside. You cannot see most of the representatives here, either. You experience both at a manageable size. With time and training, an ambassador can control their own filters of perception to specifically include the colleagues they intend to interact with. If your world had bothered to establish a proper Ambassador Academy before now, then you would have had the necessary perception training already."

"Sorry," said Gabe, though he wasn't. Not at all. He was not in the mood to apologize for his planet.

"So am I," said Protocol. "Given your lack of training, your Envoy should have given you more instruction between Embassy visits."

"We've been busy," said Gabe, without further apology.

"I see," said Protocol. "Whom are you looking for?"

Assassins, Gabe thought, but didn't say.

"I need to talk to my neighbors," he said aloud. *Space travel takes a long time and a lot of effort,* he thought. *The Envoy said so, and I knew that already. So I agree with Sapi.*

Whoever is lurking in the system is probably from around here somewhere.

"Delegates from systems adjacent to your own?" Protocol asked, clarifying.

"Yes," said Gabe.

"You might consider calling for a local match," Protocol suggested, though he also sounded doubtful. "In that case, summons will be sent to representatives of every civilization within a certain minimal distance of your own. Once gathered together, you will all play a game of your choosing. By tradition whoever calls the match selects the game. During play you will discuss whatever matters you consider important. Many clusters and constellations of ambassadors meet regularly to resume games of long standing. Your sector of the galaxy, however, does not."

"Can I request a match?" Gabe asked.

"You may," said Protocol, "though I recommend that you avoid doing so."

"Why?"

The room paused as though very carefully choosing its translated response. "It is not for me to tell you why. It is not my place to comment on the actions of civilizations represented here. I am the place itself and not an ambassador. I am only the protocol by which ambassadors meet to share information and make their own decisions. The purpose of this Embassy is to grant representative communication to everyone capable of communicating within a single galaxy. I am a conduit of information, not a source."

The room clearly wanted to say more, even though it also thought that it shouldn't.

"But?" Gabe prompted.

"But you might consider asking your colleagues about the Outlast," the room told him, still uncomfortable.

Them again, Gabe thought. "Thank you," he said out loud. "I will." He tried to be extra formal and official. Protocol loved formality—it was the nature of Protocol to love formality. "And I apologize for asking you to step out of place."

"Accepted," said the room, sounding mollified. "I understand that you do lack the proper training. Allowances must be made on your behalf."

Gabe sidestepped the room's condescension. "So if I shouldn't call for a local match, and I don't know how to notice specific people, how can I find and talk to my neighbors? The Chancery is crowded."

"It is certainly crowded," said Protocol proudly. "It is a place of infinite diversity in infinite combinations. Even if a significant percentage of the galaxy is currently experiencing mass extinctions, the Chancery is still very crowded."

"Wait, what was that?" Gabe asked, alarmed. "Mass extinctions? That sounds bad."

"I am sure it is unpleasant for those involved," Protocol agreed.

"Why is it happening?"

"That is not for me to say," Protocol told him.

Gabe swallowed his frustration. It took effort. It stuck in his throat. *My parents are in prison because they're from Mexico,* he thought. *My house lost a fight with a black hole. If the galaxy itself is burning down, then I'd appreciate it if you gave me a heads-up.* But he didn't say any of that out loud.

Protocol changed the subject. "As for your request to speak with the representatives of civilizations most proximate to your own, I can help you locate three of your closest neighbors—those native to planets within the Centauri cluster. All three are currently entangled and conversing together. I will guide you to them."

The lights dimmed—a clear hint that Gabe should leave. He could hardly see anything other than the doorway.

"Thank you, Protocol," said Gabe.

"You are welcome, Ambassador Fuentes," said the darkened room around him.

* * * *

The Chancery weather had changed since Gabe's first visit. There were more clouds, and the light shining down from each corner of the indoor sky took on new colors. It didn't seem like any particular time of day, with no rising or setting sun to measure time with. It just seemed different.

One cloud changed shape to become a great big arrow. It hovered above three ambassadors who stood clustered together near the tree line. They didn't seem to notice a huge cloud-arrow hanging in the sky and pointing at them.

"Subtle," said Gabe. "Thanks, Protocol."

He climbed down from the hills and approached the floating arrow.

An elaborate ball game unfolded over his head, played by flying and hovering ambassadors. It might have been an attempt to make a large and interactive map of several solar systems, or it might have been some kind of space soccer. No one used their hands to catch the ball, which made it look a bit like soccer—but they also avoided using their feet or wings or whatever limbs they happened to have. The players whacked the ball back and forth with the side of their hips. It looked difficult and painful.

A long line of other kids sat whispering together. Ripples of laughter ran up and down the line. *They're playing telephone,* Gabe realized. *That must be especially strange and hilarious with so many translations involved.*

He approached the three kids beneath the big orange arrow. The arrow cloud dissipated as he drew near. Then he stopped, unsure how to introduce himself.

The tallest one, a girl, held a broken branch. The two smaller kids looked boyish. All three took turns plucking leaves, folding leaf-paper airplanes like the one Gabe had made earlier, and then throwing them. They spoke low, whispering to each other. All of them wore simple orange robes.

Gabe squinted, just for a moment, to see how they saw themselves. Their shapes shifted. The tall girl looked like an eel with an entire cat for a head. One of the smaller boys looked like an armadillo made out of jellyfish. The other one resembled a tangle of tree roots and elephant ears.

Gabe immediately regretted the squint. He opened his eyes wide and tried to forget about what he had just seen, tried to trust the translation in order to more comfortably communicate and introduce himself. He still felt awkward about barging up and saying hello—especially since one of these three kids might be trying to kill him.

The other ambassadors noticed him and all turned to stare.

Gabe held up one hand. He hoped the gesture translated well.

"Hello," he said. "I'm Gabe."

Are any of you surprised to see that I'm still alive? he wondered.

The tall girl stepped forward, immediately taking charge as though she were the oldest as well as the biggest. Her hair trailed all the way down to the ground. "Hello. I'm Jir of the Builders and the Yards." She pointed to one of the boys. "This is Ca'tth, Seventeenth in the Unbroken Line."

Gabe wished he had used a more full and formal name to introduce himself. *Hello, everyone. I am Gabriel Sandro Fuentes of Terra. Or maybe Gabriel the Guardian of Lizard, Bird, and Fox. Except I had to abandon those three in Frankie's kitchen, so if that was my official role, then I've already failed it.*

He nodded to Ca'tth and tried not to think of him as Jelly Armadillo. *I really shouldn't have squinted,* he thought.

Ca'tth said nothing. His translated appearance was completely bald, and his eyes shimmered strangely. The look he gave Gabe was wary, suspicious, and unwelcoming.

Jir of the Builders and the Yards pointed at the third ambassador.

"This is Ripe-Fruit-Dropped-in-Sunbaked-Mud-and-Left-to-Sit-Content. It's his child name. His scent will change after puberty, when he settles and puts down more permanent roots, and then his name will change with it. He goes by Ripe for short, and he might not really notice you if your species doesn't have a developed sense of smell or a memorably translated scent of your own. Don't be offended if he ignores you. He doesn't mean to be rude."

"He's a *plant?*" Gabe asked, surprised.

"He's flora, yes," said Jir.

"Doesn't he mind tearing leaves off another plant?"

"No," said Jir, politely annoyed. "This is a game. It's a translated plant. And I think he cooks and eats other plants, where he comes from."

Ripe had messy hair that waved and twisted by itself. He folded a new leaf-paper airplane without acknowledging Gabe. It did seem more absentminded than rude. *I must not have a very memorable smell,* Gabe thought.

He remembered his mother's powerful sense of smell while she was pregnant with the twins. She could recognize family members by scent rather than sight or sound, so she became impossible to sneak up on. This had seemed like a superpower to Gabe, like something she could've used to fight crime. He figured that detectives should *always* be pregnant, the better to sniff out evildoers. Mom had been less excited about her temporary powers, though, and Dad had had to change all his recipes to avoid cooking up kitchen smells that nauseated her. It was the only time he had ever seemed flustered about which spices to use.

Gabe gently set the memory aside. Then he shut a mental door on that memory, locked the door, and hid the key.

Ripe tossed his folded glider. It didn't go far.

"Can I play?" Gabe asked. The whole playground setup really was useful. It gave them something to do and a way to interact, even when they weren't sure what to say to each other. He reached for the branch to pluck a leaf of his own.

"No," said Ca'tth immediately. "No, no, no, no, no." He kept his eyes fixed on Gabe while shaking his head, which was unsettling to see.

"Maybe later," said Jir, still polite, still annoyed. She sounded like a babysitter who wasn't getting paid enough for the job. "This is a private game. We live in overlapping systems, so we have shared concerns to discuss while we play."

"Then maybe I *should* join in," said Gabe—also polite, and not wanting to intrude, but not willing to leave, either. "Protocol says that we're neighbors, so we might have some of the same things to talk about."

He would have done this differently if not in a hurry. He would have waited, observed, sorted out the politics and learned how to navigate them—just as he might have done in any other kind of playground. It's important to know who hates to share the swings. It's good to figure out which bullies find fart jokes funny, and whether you can get them to stop throwing rocks by telling one. Gabe would have tried to make friends slowly, to figure out where he was welcome before barging into a group and a game uninvited. But he didn't have time for that. Someone was shooting at him. His sleeping self hid underneath a bridge. He needed to hurry.

The other three ambassadors looked alarmed at the news that they were neighbors.

"Send him away," Ca'tth whispered, urgent. His shimmering eyes grew very wide, and he tugged at Jir's sleeve with both hands. "Send the Gabe away now. Quick. Do it. Send away the Gabe."

"Just keep playing!" Jir told him in a loud, urgent whisper. "Focus! We might attract his attention if we stop playing. Fold another leaf."

"Whose attention?" Gabe asked.

The three all busied themselves with folding gliders. They pretended that they hadn't heard him. Gabe looked around.

Omegan of the Outlast stood on a hilltop nearby. Gabe remembered the phrase *mass extinctions*.

"Don't look at the Outlast!" Ca'tth hissed. His eyes grew wide enough to take up most of his face, and his ears began to flutter up and down. "Don't ever, ever, ever, ever, ever look at the Outlast. And please go away."

His voice rose and fell whenever he said a word over and over, from whisper to loud and then back down to whisper with every *ever*.

Gabe didn't protest or bother to argue. Instead he took one slow step closer, plucked his own leaf, and threw his own airplane. It flew a long way.

Jir sighed. "Maybe he should stay," she said, though she still sounded like a babysitter with better things to do. "He might hurt us more out of ignorant blundering than by knowing our business. He should learn enough to keep quiet. And he might be able to contribute somehow."

"No, no, no, no, no," Ca'tth insisted. His ears still fluttered like an agitated moth. "He can't help us. He's brand-new, and he can't travel far. We would have noticed his people already if they could, and we haven't, so they can't."

He folded a glider and threw it hard. It did not travel far either.

Ca'tth's aggressive nervousness and distaste made Gabe suspicious. *Why exactly are you trying to get rid of me?* he thought. *Why do you want me to go away? Did you recognize me? Did you expect me to be crushed inside a clothes dryer rather than here?*

Ripe sat down. He made several gliders and set them all on the ground beside him. "This is a meal," he said. "This is all a cooking cake inside an oven-cave with worms alive inside it. This is the sort of cake that might eat everyone else slowly after they digest it."

Gabe was not sure what that meant or whether it might be suspicious.

"The newcomer is still more dangerous to us ignorant than he is knowing," said Jir. She folded two gliders and tossed them together, one from each hand. They spun around each other in a double spiral before drifting apart. "And his system is close. This matters to him, too."

"No, no, no," Ca'tth protested, but he spoke softly as though already resigned to losing the argument. "Don't let him know about things he can't ever escape. Cruel, cruel, cruel, cruel, cruel. It's too cruel of us to tell him."

"Tell me what?" Gabe demanded, though he tried to keep his voice low and quiet.

Jir lashed her long hair behind her.

"Evacuation," she said.

Ca'tth groaned. Ripe sniffed the air. Jir ignored them both.

"We're planning to evacuate our systems," she went on. "That's what we're talking about here. That's what we're trying to do. The Outlast is expanding suddenly and impossibly fast. They've claimed much of their spiral arm already, and now they've begun to invade our own smaller arm. So we plan to abandon our homes. But we're not sure how to do it or where to go. Should we travel together like the Kaen, all in one nomadic fleet, or should we split up and scatter? Do we tell each other which way we're going or try to stay safe by staying secret? Do we hide and then try to find our way home again later? Do we risk uprooting Ripe's elders so they can travel, or should his people send only seedpod ships? Do we ask the Machinae for help?"

Ca'tth shook his head several times. "The Machinae never listen, never, never, never. No one understands them. And once we leave, we can never go back, not after the Outlast lays claim to our system. Then it all belongs to them, always, always, always, from now until the universe collapses on itself."

"That's only what they believe," said Jir. Her hair snapped like a whip.

"Yes," Ca'tth said sadly, "and they've been right so far." He gave up on the glider he was trying to fold, crumpled it, and threw away the crumpled ball.

Gabe plucked another leaf. "Your plane will fly better if you fold the wing tips," he told Ca'tth. "Like this."

Ca'tth and Jir both watched him fold. Ripe stayed where he sat and stuck each of his gliders in the ground, point-first, playing his own private game according to his own rules.

"How far can you travel?" Jir asked Gabe. "Have your people explored much beyond your motherworld yet?"

"Only as far as our moon," Gabe answered—a simple, honest answer. He tried not to sound defensive about it.

"Your own moon?" Jir asked. "In orbit around your own world? No farther than that?"

"Not *yet*," said Gabe. "But we have sent probes and robots farther out. There's a robot on Mars that we dropped with a sky crane. Dad and I stayed up late to watch it happen."

"I don't think you can help us," Jir told him. She still sounded condescending, but not so annoyed. "And I don't think we can help you, either. But if you haven't traveled far, then the Outlast might not even notice your people."

Ca'tth made a sudden noise that didn't translate. He snatched away the leaf branch and stomped on it.

"Hey!" said Jir, surprised and annoyed again.

"Bones and carapaces!" Ripe protested.

"Run," Ca'tth whispered, his eyes wide and his ears moving. "Omegan is watching us. Watching, watching, watching now. I'll stomp off like a sore loser. Everyone scatter. Play a chase game in the trees until we can meet again." He locked his massive eyes on Gabe. "I'm sorry," he said. "You can't travel, and we can't take you with us. Try to hide when they reach your system. I hope they don't find you."

He disappeared into the trees. Ripe followed, lifting his legs very high as he ran.

Jir of the Builders and the Yards hesitated. Her hair lashed like the long eel-ish tail that it actually was. "Farewell, Ambassador Gabe," she said. Then she walked away rather than running, though she walked quickly.

Gabe stood bewildered on the edge of the forest, alone.

Ca'tth told me to hide, he thought. *And he didn't want to frighten me with news about huge and scary things. That makes me less suspicious of him. If my neighbors are all ditching this part of the galaxy, then they probably don't have any interest in my system. Unless they want to hide out there. But it sounds like the Outlast are coming my way too. Maybe the Outlast are the ones trying to kill me—though they seem to want to kill everyone, so they're more likely to stage a massive invasion than carry out sneaky and secret assassination attempts. They're pirates, not ninjas.*

A galactic invasion inflicting mass extinctions felt like a force of nature, like tornadoes and hurricanes, like something Gabe could do nothing about other than buckle down and keep away from windows. And he still didn't know what to think about his neighbors.

He threw one last glider, frustrated. He threw it too hard and it nose-dived.

Gabe turned around to find Omegan of the Outlast standing directly beside him. He made an involuntary noise of alarm.

"Be silent," Omegan said without looking directly at Gabe. The ambassador's voice was as sharp and precise as little squares of broken windshield glass. His skin, eyes, and hair were all extremely pale, almost transparent. His expression was less transparent—Gabe saw nothing through it, nothing of what the other ambassador might think or intend to do. "You *must* be silent," Omegan said again, his voice less sharp this time. "You must say nothing about your world or capabilities, not where I can hear you. I must not learn these things. Tell me that you understand."

Not really, Gabe admitted to himself, but he said, "Yes," anyway.

Omegan of the Outlast seemed satisfied, and he walked back to his hilltop.

Gabe felt a huge headache coming on, fed by his incomprehension. *He gave me a warning. About himself. Not a threat—a warning. Why would he do that?*

A crumpled leaf-ball missed his face. He looked up. Sapi crouched on a tree branch. Kaen stood on the same branch, balanced without holding on. She looked extra-serious.

"Stupid!" Sapi yelled. "Didn't I warn you about the Outlast? Can your species even make long-term memories?"

Gabe didn't have time to respond. Dizziness wrenched him away from his sense of entangled self.

I'm waking up, he realized. *I must be under attack.*

13

Gabe was not under attack, but he was underwater. He came sputtering to the surface and found himself still under a bridge.

It was dark. He could see reflected moonlight in the pool beneath the waterfall. This time he actually felt rested.

"Sorry," the Envoy said from the rock above. "My apologies. *Mea culpa.* I am culpable in your soaking. I tried to wake you before you fell in, but I couldn't. With time and practice it should become easier to transition between your waking life and entangled travel. I hope that you will actually have the time to practice."

Gabe climbed back onto the rock. "Me too," he said, shivering. The water was cold. The rock was cold, too. He pulled off his clothes and wrung them out, one piece at a time. Then he dried himself off with a small camping towel from his emergency backpack and put his clothes back on.

"What did you learn?" the Envoy asked. "Did anyone seem surprised to see you? Did they try to find out where you are?"

"Not really," said Gabe. "Pretty much the opposite." He described the Embassy visit while rubbing his hair with the towel and trying to get water out of his ears.

The Envoy listened. It shifted between different shades of purple as it listened.

"So that's it," said Gabe. "Our neighbors claim to be leaving, and they didn't seem to want anything to do with me. So we still don't know who is shooting at us, and we have to worry about an Outlast invasion, and I don't understand what Omegan tried to warn me about. I didn't always understand the neighbors, either. The plant made no sense to me at all. Even translated, he still didn't make any sense."

Gabe had a thought that he didn't like and didn't want to say aloud. But the Envoy remained an expectant shade of purple, so Gabe kept talking. "What if . . . What if the aliens shooting at us are *completely* alien to me? What if I can't ever understand why they're doing this? How can I stop them if I can't translate what they want? I don't even get most of my own species. Frankie's mom makes no sense to me either. I can't tell how she feels about anything."

"Breathe, ambassador," said the Envoy in an excellent imitation of Mom's most soothing voice.

Gabe took a breath. This took effort.

"Whatever else occurs," the Envoy said, slowly and still soothing, "you should trust in translation. Life anywhere and everywhere has very much in common. The nature of survival makes sure this is true. And social creatures enjoy and require communication. Understanding might be difficult, but it is possible. Always."

Gabe nodded. He tried to convince his breath and pulse to both relax into a steadier rhythm. He tried not to pay attention to simmering discomfort way down at the foundations of himself.

The Envoy took a new breath of its own and held it for a bit before speaking. "What I still don't understand is how the Outlast could be moving so quickly. It should have taken them thousands of years to spread so far. The previous ambassador was concerned about this. It's why she left this system."

"What happened to the previous ambassador?" Gabe asked.

"I wish I knew," the Envoy admitted.

Gabe spread out the towel on the cold, clammy rock, hoping it would dry.

"Tell me more about the Outlast," he said. "How are they even allowed to join the Embassy if they go around conquering planets and killing off other civilizations?"

"*Everyone* is allowed to join the Embassy, Gabe," said the Envoy. "It is surprising that the Outlast bothers to send an ambassador, given how little they regard other forms of life, but everyone is allowed. The Outlast intends to be the only sentient species left standing when the universe collapses. They believe that the end of one cosmos will lead to the birth of another, and that the next one can be shaped by whoever is still around when it happens. So they mean to be the only ones left. But they used to be content to just wait until the end came, assuming that everyone else would die off by then. Now they seem less patient. I would have told you about them earlier, but we haven't had much opportunity to prepare you between Embassy visits."

"Protocol is still pretty grumpy about that," said Gabe.

"I'm sure," said the Envoy. It sounded like it would be rolling its eyes if it had separate eyes to roll.

Gabe fished out a package of *Galletas Marías* as a midnight snack. He chewed the cookies in a slow and thoughtful way, chewing over new information at the same time.

A faint electronic noise chirped somewhere nearby.

Gabe flinched. At first he thought it might be some sort of alien drone seeking him out. Then he realized it was coming from the outer pocket of his backpack.

Gabe dug out his cheap cell phone. He had missed a couple of calls, followed by a single text from Lupe. The little screen glowed in the dark beneath the bridge.

It's late. Why aren't you back yet? Mom's back. I told her you went to bed early, in Frankie's room, so she doesn't know you aren't here. She went to bed early, too. But the twins are up. My arms are full of twins. One of them is trying to eat my phone RIGHT NOW. Where are you and why aren't you here?

I'm fine, he wrote. Don't worry about me. He didn't tell her that he was hiding under a bridge or that he couldn't risk coming back to Frankie's house because he didn't want energy beams to burn through the sky and ceiling while he was there.

Come back, she answered immediately. Now, please. I'm not worried about you. I'm worried about Mom. She needs you here. So do the twins.

Can't come back yet, he typed. Still doing secret stuff.

Lupe texted scathing and terrible things at him.

Gabe responded with smiling emoticons.

Fine, she wrote. How's the planet?

Still here, he typed.

Good job. Tell the purple goo to keep you safe. Get back here ASAP.

Ok.

He wondered how long that would be. Then he forced himself to stop wondering, finished his cookies, and mulled over galactic genocide.

"I don't think the Outlast is after us," he said. "Not yet, anyway."

"Agreed," said the Envoy. "They wouldn't bother with secret assassinations. And they might not even notice this world, given that Terrans are barely spacefaring. It seems more likely that the Outlast would focus their conquering attention on civilizations that take up more space. We may yet remain safely outside that attention."

Gabe nodded. "That's pretty much what Sapi said. And Ca'tth. And Omegan himself told me not to tell him anything. He agrees that I should avoid catching his attention, which is odd. I don't understand why. And I haven't learned anything about those ships in the asteroid belt or the one shooting at us, and we can't stay down here forever." He rubbed his arms, shivering. Even summer nights could be cold in Minneapolis—especially underneath a bridge.

"We shouldn't stay here," the Envoy agreed. "Your

enemies, whoever they are, can track your location. It's dangerous to remain in any one place for long."

While he packed his few belongings and put his damp sneakers back on, Gabe tried to think of where they might run to next. Downtown had larger buildings and more shelter, but it also had far more people in it. He didn't want anyone else caught in the blast when the next attack found him.

It would make sense to stay on buses and trains to keep in constant motion, just to be a moving target. Destinations and directions wouldn't matter. But he didn't have enough money to buy transit tickets forever, and neither the buses nor the trains would run all night.

"Is there any way to block the entanglement signal, to keep them from tracking us?" Gabe asked. "Should I wrap myself in tin foil?"

"No," the Envoy told him. "It would do you no good to wrap yourself in tin foil."

The ground beneath them moved. Boulders in the stream bed shifted. Gabe grabbed the one they sat on with both arms.

The ground held still.

Gabe also held himself very still.

"Is that what a landing spacecraft would feel like?" he asked, his voice low.

The Envoy shook its mouth. "That came from *below us*, which makes very little sense to me."

The boulder beneath them rumbled again. Gabe felt fear scrape his insides. He took up his great-grandfather's cane and reached for his backpack.

The stone cliff beside the waterfall broke apart. A metal shape emerged. It looked like a basement silverfish grown to dragon-size, with dozens of legs extending from joints all along its length.

Several legs pushed outward from the cliff face. The burrowing craft lowered itself and peered beneath the bridge through waterfall spray. A red disk glowed like a single eye at the very front.

"You should run, Ambassador," the Envoy said.

Gabe ducked and scrambled behind the boulder.

A beam of burning light swept through the space beneath the bridge and severed the Envoy's throat. Puppetish limb and body slid off the rock in two separate directions. The Envoy's mouth still moved, still tried to speak as it dropped into the water and sank.

14

Gabe did not move. He no longer knew how to move.

The boulder broke apart, and then Gabe moved very quickly.

He scrambled between the stones to get back to shore. One foot slipped into the water and suddenly became much colder than his other foot. He climbed the railing to the hiking path. His sopping sneaker squelched. The cane rattled in his hands. Both of his hands shook. They shook from the raw force of adrenaline rather than panic or fear. The scraping terror he had felt before was gone. The ache of the Envoy's loss was also gone, shut off, and set aside. Both emotions would come back later, if Gabe lived long enough to feel them, but in that moment he knew only running.

Another energy beam roasted the air nearby. A tree beside the trail burst open. The sap inside boiled as though struck by lightning.

Gabe ducked away from the spray of hot tree blood and ran harder. He moved in a haphazard way, zigzagging like Sir Toby did whenever the fox played the chase games that taught him how to hunt and how to escape when something else was hunting him.

The sinuous metal thing tore through the creek bed. It splashed water and scraped against stones, moving parallel to the hiking trail. Then it lunged forward to slide downstream ahead of Gabe. The craft turned, reared up like some sort of spitting snake, and fired another beam from the glowing red cannon at the tip. Two more trees burst and burned.

Gabe threw himself sideways, sneakers slipping against the trail. After the skid, he ran back the way he had come, back toward the falls. He wondered what he would do when he reached them.

I'm cornered, he thought. *I'll never get up those stone steps fast enough. This is a dead end.* The words *dead end* repeated in his head to the thudding beat of his sneakers on the trail. *Dead, dead, dead. End.*

He didn't actually get that far.

The alien craft surged back upstream, climbed the bank with its many legs, and blocked the trail with the length of its body.

Gabe tried to keep from slamming into it, slipped, and slammed into it anyway.

The craft coiled itself around him, a huge metal spiral with Gabe trapped in the center. It raised the front half of its length to peer down at him. The headlike shape was a cockpit, the face made out of thick and semitransparent material. Gabe couldn't see through it, couldn't tell whether there was a pilot inside—someone he could talk to, communicate with, reason with. Someone he could demand answers from. *Tell me why you're doing this.*

The craft moved slowly now, keeping Gabe trapped while it took careful aim. The coils contracted. The cockpit lowered. The cannon glowed directly above his head.

Gabe drew Toledo steel from inside his great-grandfather's cane and drove the blade up into the cannon. The red disk shattered. Arcs of energy raced up and down the length of the craft. It reared its head back and writhed.

He held on to the sword hilt, though he probably shouldn't have. The machine's whiplash motion yanked Gabe off his feet and into the air. He let go of the hilt too late and went flying like a slingshot stone.

Time almost stopped—or at least Gabe's perception of time slowed down to a careful, deliberate crawl. He saw the moon above him. It looked close enough to touch in the clear night sky.

Gabe had just enough time to think, *This is going to hurt,* before he landed in the pool at the base of the waterfall. It hurt.

Gabriel Sandro Fuentes opened his eyes. It didn't help. He couldn't see anything. He didn't know where he was. His back still stung from hitting the water.

He moved his arms and legs. This took effort, more than it should have. They moved sluggishly, the air around them very cold and oddly thick.

This isn't air, he realized. *This is water. I'm still underwater. That's bad.*

He took in a sharp, surprised breath—and noticed that he *could* breathe. Air surrounded his head, but not the rest of him. He tried to touch his face and couldn't. He touched the outside of a flexible bubble-helmet instead.

"This is weird," he said, and heard himself say. His voice sounded strange inside the bubble-helmet. Gabe had a high tolerance for weirdness, but his new circumstances still qualified as unexpectedly odd.

Shapes glowed in front of him and moved across the surface of the helmet. Scripts and hieroglyphs wrote themselves into his field of vision, brightly purple like bioluminescent jellyfish. They shifted into something more like recognizable text, though Gabe still didn't recognize it.

Вы не знаете этот язык? Я попробую иначе.

The purple color was familiar, even if the written language wasn't.

"Envoy?"

The glow vanished. New words appeared.

Hello, Gabe. Sorry about that. Apologies. Your confusion is my fault. I tried several different alphabets before remembering which one you'd be familiar with.

Gabe poked the outside of the bubble-helmet with one finger. The glowing words rippled in front of him. "This is you? You made yourself into a helmet?"

I did, the Envoy wrote on its own surface. You were briefly unconscious after impact and would have drowned. I'm sifting oxygen from the water around us and filtering out the carbon dioxide you exhale.

"Thanks," said Gabe. "I thought you were dead. I'm glad you're not." That sounded dumb to say out loud, but it was true, and he didn't know what else to say. He didn't feel capable of saying anything else. Moments ago he had been alone, completely alone, without home or family or Envoy. Now he wasn't. Every emotion his brain had set aside came back to him now. He felt them all at once. That made it very difficult to speak.

I'm not dead, the Envoy wrote. I'm also glad about that. My bodily systems are evenly distributed rather than concentrated into separate organs, so I can lose much of me and still remain myself. You're far more fragile and might be injured. How do you feel?

"Ow," Gabe answered. He crawled along the bottom of the pool and checked himself for impact injuries as he moved. He still couldn't see anything beyond the bubble-helmet of Envoy, but he could feel the water flowing downstream and away from the thunderous, bubbling froth of the waterfall. "I don't think I broke anything."

Good, the Envoy wrote. Still, you should try not to exert yourself. Move slowly. And be very careful as you leave the water. The attacking craft has not moved since you stabbed it with a sword—I would have felt the shuddering vibrations of its movement otherwise—but it might not be completely inert. It's unclear how much danger you're in at this moment.

"Do you think I killed the pilot?" Gabe asked. He was not at all sure how he felt about the possibility.

It might not have had a pilot at all, the Envoy wrote. If it did, then you may have killed it. But you should know that many forms of

LIFE HAVE A CLEAR ETHIC OF SELF-DEFENSE. THOUGH
MANY ALSO AGREE THAT VIOLENT CONFLICT HAS A
TERRIBLE AND ENTROPIC COST. I'M SORRY THAT YOU
HAVE SUFFERED THIS COST.

Gabe said nothing. He had nothing to say. He crawled
along with the current until the creek became more shallow. Then he climbed up and out, shivering. The moonlight looked purplish through his bubble-helmet.

The Envoy dropped down from his shoulders and
took up its usual shape.

"Let me investigate first," it whispered.

"Okay," Gabe whispered back. "Try not to get beheaded."

"I don't have a head," the Envoy pointed out. "But I'll
try to avoid getting bisected again."

Gabe rubbed his arms and jumped up and down, trying
to warm himself. He listened for the clanking of the alien
craft in motion, but it lay silently curled up on the trail.

Gabe also listened for shouting or sirens from above
the ravine, but he didn't hear those, either. The park was
closed. No one in the surrounding city had noticed the
fight, apparently.

He went searching for his backpack and found it.
Then he found the scorched piece of Envoy. It was down
among the rocks, oozing around as though looking for
the rest. Gabe picked it up.

"Hey!" he whispered as loudly as he dared. He glanced over his shoulder to make sure that no wounded alien pilots were sneaking up on him. "I found your missing piece!"

The Envoy didn't seem to hear him. It climbed a tree beside the trail and looked down, surveying the scene. Then it jumped away from the branch, stretched itself out, and glided in a slow spiral like a falling leaf. It landed on the inert craft. Gabe half-expected the thing to leap up and try to eat the Envoy, but it didn't move at all.

He crept closer to the trail. His sopping shoes squelched underfoot.

The Envoy oozed along the edge of the cockpit, pushing and prodding until a hatch opened. Faint lights pulsed inside.

Nothing came out. The Envoy went in.

Gabe waited for a few heartbeats, or maybe for five thousand years. He wasn't really sure which.

"Envoy? Hello? Are you okay in there?"

The Envoy's puppetish mouth popped up from inside the cockpit.

"Hello," it said. "I think we can relax for the moment. We don't seem to be in any immediate danger. The craft is automated or possibly controlled remotely. There is no pilot. Unless this smear of sooty ashes was once a pilot, but I doubt it. The ash seems to be pure carbon. That doesn't help me identify its source. Almost everyone is carbon-based. Carbon is a very useful molecule for life to use while building itself up."

Gabe held out the scorched and severed piece of Envoy. "Here," he said. "Build yourself up."

The Envoy hopped down from the craft and then tried to absorb the rest of itself. This looked difficult and possibly painful. The lost piece sat inside it, discolored and wriggling uncomfortably. Gabe looked away.

"So there's no pilot," he said. "Is there anything about the ship that you recognize? Anything that might tell us who they are?"

"I *have* figured out what the vehicle is for," the Envoy said, its voice proud and self-satisfied.

"Me too," said Gabe. "The evidence is kinda subtle, but I'm pretty sure it's an alien assassin's attack ship."

"Wrong!" said the Envoy. "It might have been *repurposed* as a weapon, but that's not its purpose by design. This is a mining craft made to harvest veins of ice. We are dealing with ice pirates, and definitely not an organized invasion force that the Outlast might employ. The cannon that you broke is an ice-cutting drill, not a gun. That's why its aim is so bad. A military device would have been better at hitting a moving target, but ice does not run away."

"It still hit you," Gabe pointed out.

"I wasn't moving," said the Envoy. "I was encouraging you to move instead. And you're welcome."

"Thank you," said Gabe, remembering what it was like to be entirely alone. "So are they mining *here*, on the planet? Is that why it was burrowing around?"

"I very much doubt it," the Envoy said. "I think it was just trying to sneak up on you. Too difficult to lift resources offworld. There's no need for them to expend all that effort. Plenty of ice in the asteroid belt, where I first noticed their ships. Much easier to find it out there. Much easier to avoid notice, too, which is clearly important to them."

"I'm not so sure," Gabe argued. "Big metal dragon-bugs don't seem sneaky to me."

"Each attack has been carefully and cautiously directed," the Envoy pointed out. "They are shooting at you—but not the whole city and not the whole planet. They must fear the attention of an ambassador who might communicate their piracy to the rest of the Embassy. They fear exposure. So it follows that your best response to these attacks would be to expose them."

"How?" Gabe asked, frustrated. "We still don't know who they are."

The Envoy grinned wide. "I think I can repair this craft," it said, excited and proud. "We can go find out."

15

Gabriel Sandro Fuentes sat in the cockpit of an alien craft, preparing to launch, when his phone beeped.

It's almost dawn! his sister wrote. WHERE ARE YOU?

Busy, he wrote back. Light a candle to St. Joseph of Cupertino for me.

Gabe's grandparents had sent him a book about the lives of saints and the grotesque things that always happened to them. The book became favorite sleepover reading whenever Frankie failed to find them a horror movie.

The crazy one? Lupe typed, far more speedily than Gabe could.

Weren't all saints crazy?

Sure, she typed, but this one is specifically a patron saint of mental handicaps.

And astronauts, Gabe pointed out.

Same difference, said Lupe.

LIGHT ME A CANDLE, he said, capitalizing each individual letter. If his phone had a caps lock, he had no idea how to turn it on.

Fine, she said. But get back here SOON. When Mom wakes up, she'll find out that you're missing. Don't do that to her. Not now. Not today.

Can't you just tell her that I have important business with aliens?

Lupe described what she intended to do to him with the rubber mallet of wisdom and truth. She typed it all out with speed, and with many typos.

Abrazos, Gabe answered, and put the phone away.

"Are you ready, Ambassador?" the Envoy asked.

Gabe didn't answer.

Dad gets deported today, he thought. *We could rescue him before it happens. We could dig under the detention center and help him escape. We could burrow through the ground rather than launch ourselves away from it. We could do that.*

He thought about other huge metal dragon-bugs tracking him, following him, shooting at him while he tried to rescue his dad, shooting at Frankie's house— again—when he tried to bring his family back together.

Gabe closed the door on that thought, nailed it shut, and piled mental furniture in front of it. To protect his family he needed to be very far away.

"Ready," he said, though he wasn't sure it was even possible to be ready for this.

The craft coiled into a spring and leaped into the air. Segments of its tail separated, spread out like propeller blades, and spun. It hovered long enough to fire a blast of fuel behind it. Steam and smoke filled the ravine at the base of Minnehaha Falls.

The craft reached escape velocity and escaped.

Gabriel Sandro Fuentes, the ambassador of his world, left it.

The back of the cockpit was curved and cushioned like a Papasan chair. Gabe lay smooshed in the center, his arms and legs splayed out around him as though modeling a da Vinci sketch of human proportions—though it was clear that the cockpit had been built with entirely different proportions in mind.

The alien vehicle fought with gravity and created more of it, making Gabe's body too heavy to move. A puddle of Envoy lay smooshed beside him. The transparent hatch glowed, bright with friction against the outside air. The glow faded when they left the atmosphere behind.

Gabe saw stars through the hatch. They no longer flickered. They burned with constant, steady light in different colors.

Overwhelming weight turned to weightlessness. Gabe's backpack and his great-grandfather's empty, hollow cane hovered beside him. The Envoy, Gabe's fellow traveler, floated by as a perfect sphere.

I'm in space, Gabe thought over and over, surrounding everything else he had to think about. *I'm in space.*

Both the world and the ship turned toward the sun. Gabe watched the sunrise. All other stars vanished in the bright, reflected earthlight.

Smaller flashes of light pulsed in displays around the otherwise dim cabin. Gabe couldn't tell what any of the information meant, or what any of the controls were for. This didn't matter too much, though. The craft operated by gesture more than touch.

The Envoy made a mouth, inhaled, and then exhaled to fly around the cabin like a slow-leaking balloon. It took in another breath to speak with.

"I wish I could act as pilot," it said, "but the motion sensors don't seem to recognize me as something substantial enough to pay attention to. I can push buttons on the dashboard, but I can't steer the vehicle itself. You'll have to be the pilot."

Gabe cracked his knuckles. "Good," he said. "How?"

"Point to where you want to go. The farther you

extend your arm, the more force the craft will put into its propulsion. Aim for the moon."

Gabe tried to steer, but it wasn't easy to control his gestures while weightless. He kept flailing, and he couldn't steady himself in the empty air. The craft flailed along with him.

"Point your arm at the moon," the Envoy told him again.

"Trying," said Gabe. "Which way is the moon?"

"Back that way," said the Envoy. "No, *that way*. Look at where my mouth is pointing. We are currently falling back toward the planet, where we'll probably crash in Antarctica."

Gabe struggled to keep the craft steady. "Maybe you should choose a penguin as the next ambassador."

The Envoy made a *phhhhhhhht* noise of annoyance, which propelled it bouncing around the cabin. "I might," it said as it tried to keep still. "I have never yet selected a penguin for the role. They are good swimmers and know how to navigate between two different worlds, above the ice and below it. A penguin might be an excellent choice. The moon is still that way."

Gabe kept his mouth shut and concentrated. He finally got the craft pointed where they needed to go.

The moon burned bright in the view ahead.

"Shouldn't we aim for where it *will be* by the time we get that far out?" he asked. "Not where it is right now?"

"If this craft moved more slowly, then yes," said the Envoy. "But it moves very fast. Extend your arm."

Gabe did. He pointed boldly. "To the moon!"

He felt himself pressed against the Papasan-ish back of the cabin, though not with smooshing force this time. Then he became weightless again, moving at the same speed as the vehicle around him.

The Envoy ballooned its way to the dashboard and pushed at the controls. "There. Now you can move around without changing our course."

"How long will it take us to get there?" Gabe asked.

"A few hours," said the Envoy. "Our destination will shift during that time, but we can chase it easily enough. Feels strange for me to be going back there so soon. I spent a long time trying to leave."

"What were you even doing there?" Gabe asked. "How did you get stranded?" He drifted off to the side of the cabin and bumped up against the wall with his shoulder. *I'm in space!* He found that he could move around just by gently poking the walls with his fingertips.

"I helped your predecessor make travel plans, and then got stuck," the Envoy said. "She negotiated passage out of our system. She was concerned about the Outlast—for all the same reasons that you are concerned about the Outlast, though they had not spread so far then—and she thought she could best protect this world by leaving it."

Gabe thought he heard disapproval in the Envoy's voice. "We just left it too," he pointed out.

"But we're not going nearly as far away as she did," the Envoy said.

It spent most of their transit time telling Gabe about Nadia, the previous ambassador. She lived in Moscow. Her family was Jewish and tried to hide it most of the time. An ambassador always knows how to belong to more than one world at once.

Nadia had an uncle working in the Soviet space program—or programs, really. There were more than one, and not all of them were on speaking terms with each other. Her uncle helped design the Zvezda moon base, and that turned out to be useful for Ambassador Nadia. She needed neutral territory, an off-world place to meet and negotiate in person.

"The Russian program intended to create a permanent base," the Envoy explained. "A shelter that would grow into an entire city. It looked as though they would manage it. They put the first probe in space, sent the first probe into orbit around the moon, took the first pictures of the far side, and remotely managed the first robotic landing there. They meant to send people there first, and then actually live on the surface—not just plant a flag and whack a couple of golf balls. But to the American program, the moon was a conquest to be wooed and abandoned after winning the race. Russian programs had more faithful plans."

"Hey," Gabe interrupted, annoyed. "Don't knock NASA."

"Hmph," said the Envoy. "Your pardon. Apologies. Sorry." It didn't really sound sorry. "I remember that competition from the other side of it. In any case, dreams of lunar cities fizzled after the Americans landed. Most of the Russian programs shifted their ambitions and started to make orbiting space stations instead. But they still dropped separate modules of the Zvezda base on the moon's far side. They put it together remotely with radio signals and rolling Lunokhod robots. Then Ambassador Nadia and I stowed away on the last of the N-1 rockets. That was in 1974. The launch was difficult and much less comfortable than our liftoff this morning. We had to toss out equipment of precisely the same weight in order to fit, and we almost exploded right after launch. Our return lander was damaged. I only figured that out later, and by then Ambassador Nadia had left the system. I stayed stranded on the moon. That wasn't her fault.

She didn't know. While there, I modified and improved the Zvezda observatory equipment, which is how I first noticed the intruding ships in the asteroid belt. We can use the same equipment to track them more precisely."

Gabe waved his arm to interrupt. Something else had become suddenly urgent.

"Does this little ship have a bathroom?" he asked.

"No, I don't think so," said the Envoy. "The anatomy of those who built it might not require a bathroom. Or else they might wear suits with built-in waste collection. Nadia wore a large diaper on our lunar trip." It paused. "She'd be unhappy to know that I shared this information."

Gabe took a deep breath and let it slowly out.

"How badly do you need a bathroom?" the Envoy asked. "Can you wait? The base has crude facilities, and a little gravity will make the process easier."

"I don't think I can wait," said Gabe. "This is urgent. Suddenly. With no warning."

"Not surprising," said the Envoy. "The weight of urine collecting in your bladder is what tells you it's there. But neither your bladder nor anything inside it has noticeable weight right now."

"Makes sense," said Gabe, pained and clenched. "So what can I do?"

He ended up making a makeshift toilet out of a plastic

bag and his camping towel. He needed the towel to soak up pee inside the bag—otherwise floating streams of the stuff would have bounced out again with equal and opposite force.

Gabe felt a bit embarrassed to do this in front of the Envoy, who still sounded like his mother. "Turn away, please," he asked midstream.

"I can't," said the Envoy. "All of me is an eye. I could point my mouth away from you, but every part of my surface can still see."

"Fine," said Gabe.

One splash did escape. It formed a perfect pee sphere. Gabe reached out with the plastic bag, caught the globule inside, and then tied the bag tightly shut.

"Nicely done," said the Envoy. "That was a decent piece of astroengineering on the fly."

"Ha," said Gabe. "So, you were saying we can track the ice pirates from the moon base." *That was kind of fun to say out loud,* he thought.

"Yes," said the Envoy. "They clearly fear discovery. Let's go discover them."

PART FOUR
ENTRUSTED

16

The lunar surface loomed large in Gabe's view.

"Keep the nose up," the Envoy told him. "We must reach the far side, just beyond the landing site for the *Luna 24* probe—which you probably can't see from here, so never mind. That side is dark at the moment. Hopefully our headlamps will give us enough light to land by."

Gabe moved his outstretched arm to shift the angle of their descending orbit. They crossed the lit horizon and flew behind the full moon. It was extremely dark. Gabe saw precisely nothing of the ground in front of them.

"What headlamps?" he asked in a whisper. It seemed important to whisper while this close to the moon. "Could you turn them on?"

"They're on already," the Envoy told him in a worried whisper of its own. "Can't you see them? I can see them.

Maybe the alien pilot used a different spectrum of light to see by—a wavelength invisible to you."

"I can't see anything but the glowing parts of the dashboard," said Gabe.

The Envoy pushed a few dashboard buttons. "Can you see now?"

"No." Gabe glared at the absolute darkness of the ground below. He had no idea how close it was, no idea when they might slam into it. "Now I wish you could drive."

"Me too," said the Envoy. "This landing is going to be difficult. Please pull up—not that much—and now steer a little to the left to avoid a series of sharp mountain peaks. Yes, good. Good."

"My nose itches," said Gabe.

"Do not scratch your nose!" said the Envoy. "Please don't distract the motion guidance of this craft by scratching your nose."

Gabe scrunched up his face and tried to keep his outstretched hand steady.

"Extend your other arm in the opposite direction," the Envoy instructed. "Then bring it forward and open that hand."

He did. The craft cranked its tail around to fire its engines ahead of them, slowing their descent. The engine blast cast a dim, blue light. Gabe saw the ground leap at him. He flinched. He almost threw both hands in front of his face by reflex, but he didn't.

"Close your left hand. Open it one more time, briefly. Now point it behind you again."

He did. Darkness returned. Gabe tried to blink away the afterimage of the ground, tried to guess how close to it they were.

"We are about to slide across the floor of a shallow crater," the Envoy told him, whispering again. "Hopefully we will do so without bouncing much. The legs of the craft should grab the ground automatically." It pushed two buttons. "Since there are no handholds or seat belts, I recommend curling up in a fetal position . . . now."

Gabe tried to make himself into a ball. Then he felt like someone was hitting him from all directions at once. He knew what was actually happening. He knew that he was tumbling around the inside of the cabin, bouncing off the walls. But it didn't feel like he was moving at all. Everything else was moving and pummeling him.

The craft tumbled and scraped to a long, slow stop.

Gabe uncurled himself and pushed back into the Papasan-like chair. He settled downward. He had landed on the moon. He now had a "down" to settle toward.

He listened for hissing sounds and held out his hand

to feel for drafts, afraid they might have sprung a leak in the rough landing. The dim lights of the cabin display were still on, filled with information that Gabe couldn't read. And he still couldn't see anything outside. The cabin angled toward the ground. If the headlamps were on, Gabe still couldn't see them. Instead of moon rock, Gabe saw the Envoy smooshed up against the windshield.

"You okay?" he asked.

The Envoy peeled itself away from the transparent surface, drifted down, and made a mouth.

"Fascinating . . . ," it said. It hopped in place and then stretched out its neck to peer outside. Its voice sounded higher with its throat stretched so thin. "You picked a very interesting place to land."

Gabe moved to stand beside the Envoy. He wasn't weightless now, but he had only a fraction of his usual weight. "I think the place picked us rather than the other way around," he said. "What's so fascinating about it? I still can't see anything out there."

"I might be able to fix that," said the Envoy. It pushed more pieces of the dashboard display around. "Maybe. I should have tried this earlier. . . . Oh, dear. Oops."

"What's wrong?" Gabe demanded.

"That landing damaged the craft," said the Envoy. "We

should be able to move across the lunar surface, but I very much doubt we can launch again."

"So we're stuck here," said Gabe.

"I'm sure we'll think of something," the Envoy said, trying to be cheerful. "And at least I can adjust the lights."

The view outside became visible to Gabe—dim at first and then brighter.

A field of oddly shaped stones stretched out in front of them.

He saw that the stones were brightly colored rather than lunar gray.

He saw that they were not stones.

"This can't . . . ," he started to say. "This isn't . . ." He gave up. His mind hadn't rebelled against the sight of the Envoy or the sight of the mining ship come to kill him or even the sight of the Embassy and his own alien colleagues when he squinted at their actual shapes. But his mind rebelled now.

He saw dinosaurs, each one crested with three horns. Several triceratops lay dead on the surface of the moon.

"Fascinating," the Envoy said again, its neck craned thin to peer over the edge of the display. "The comet impact was very severe, I remember. It must have knocked this herd off-world entirely. Then they drifted until lunar gravity caught them up and brought them back down."

Gabe nodded slowly without really listening. Then he listened.

"Wait," he said. "Wait just a moment."

"I'm waiting," said the Envoy.

"You *remember*? You remember the comet? The one that smacked into the Gulf of Mexico? You were there?"

"I was," said the Envoy. "I don't remember very much from that era. Memory is always an uncertain thing, salvaged and bent into whatever we need it to be, and those old memories are worn especially thin. But I do remember the comet. It was memorable."

Gabe began to realize just how little he knew about the Envoy. "Where did you come from?" he asked.

"Here," it answered. "Not this moon, but this planet. Yours. Instructions for making Envoys out of local material are sent in seedpods to every system and habitable world. I was born here. I've never lived anywhere else. I have no species of my own, no genetic family heritage to share with the rest of Terran life, but otherwise I'm as native to this place as you are—and as native as they were."

Gabe returned his attention to the triceratops. They had always been his favorite dinosaur—less aggressive than faster and toothier beasts, but no less badass. They looked like knights with helmets, shields, and swords already a part of them. He imagined triceratops minding their own business, never looking for trouble, but always able to handle trouble whenever it came looking for them.

His encyclopedic book of dinosaurs back home had pictures of lumpy, orange triceratops, but the ones in front of him had bright and feathery scales. Each helmet crest displayed blue-and-green patterns that reminded him of a peacock's tail.

The dinosaur book that I used *to have at home,* Gabe corrected himself. He had seen it on the floor, scattered with the others, when he'd pulled Garuda through his bedroom window and shouted for Sir Toby. He wanted that book back now, even though the pictures in it were wrong, even though triceratops skin was neither dull nor orange. They wore bright and brilliant colors. And they were here, right here, vacuum-preserved. But they were also dead, all of them, their feather-scales scorched by friction with the air when they'd left it, their eyes gone from the sudden pressure drop to nothing at all. They reminded Gabe of the bodies he imagined Sophia the non-exchange-student had seen in the desert, dead and a long way from home.

He leaned closer to the windshield. Above the lunar horizon he could see the Earth hovering. They must have gotten turned around in the tumbled landing, and now faced home. It looked small. A planet might seem like solid ground while you happen to be standing on it, but still it moves.

Gabe tried to make out the shape of continents. He tried to remember the relative positions of Minneapolis and Guadalajara. Instead he saw mostly clouds. The globe hovering in front of him was too small to show any such detail. Gabe couldn't even tell which hemisphere he was looking at. The world wasn't a map. It didn't bother to indicate borders, boundaries, or place names. It didn't show him the line that his father would be exiled across. Today. Now. Right at that moment.

"We should be moving," the Envoy finally said. "The Zvezda base is in that direction, around to the far side and away from the Earth."

Gabe nodded.

He found it easier to direct the alien craft now that he had some gravity to work with. It helped him keep his arms steady while finding the right gestures.

The craft extended legs and hoisted itself up to a skittering, silverfish-like position. Gabe steered carefully through the triceratops graveyard and across fields of gray dust and stone.

17

Zvezda Base was a series of cylindrical, beige pods. Each pod sat on eight wheels and looked like a large vitamin.

Gabe thought about how much his father hated vitamins. The man despised the whole idea of vitamins. They were nutrients stripped all the way down to the bare-bones geometry of survival—tiny, sterile, swallowable food without any actual meal involved. No cooking. No mess. No friends and family laughing or arguing around the dinner table. Just a pill. Dad refused to take vitamins, ever, even when snotty colds took over the household and Mom tried to push vitamin C on everyone. "It's just the inside rind of an orange peel," he'd protest. "And I would rather eat orange peels." Then he *would* eat orange peels while Mom grumbled and made everyone else take vitamins.

Gabe tried not to think about his family.

"This place doesn't look like much," he said out loud. This was bare-bones survival, the vitamin equivalent of house and home. He hadn't really expected to find a gleaming silver city on the far side of the moon, but he still felt disappointed. Zvezda looked abandoned, left on cinder blocks in Earth's backyard.

"It's a remarkable achievement, actually," said the Envoy, sounding miffed. "You should be more impressed."

Gabe lifted one hand to steer the alien craft closer.

"Why is it half buried?" he asked. Drifts of gray moon dust covered several pods on one side, like windblown snow—but there was no wind out here to move the dust around.

"The soil is an extra layer of protection against small meteors," the Envoy explained. "Most of the base was supposed to be buried. But the robotic shovel broke half-way through the burial process."

"I'm feeling more and more confident about this place," said Gabe.

"Ai, hush," said the Envoy, sounding very much like Mom. "The front door is over there."

Gabe inched the craft forward. They passed the Envoy's escape cannon and approached the entrance pod. This one was entirely unburied, with blue and gray stripes decorating the side and a big round hatch at the end.

Gabe stared at the hatch.

"How do I get in?" he asked. "I don't have a suit. Should I just hold my breath and run?"

"No," said the Envoy. "You shouldn't hold your breath and run. We will have to hurry, but this is going to be much more difficult for me than for you. I can protect you from the cold and the vacuum, but given the pressure difference, it will take a lot of effort to stay flexible. I'll have to stretch myself extremely thin, and you won't have much breath to spare."

Gabe climbed down from the open hatch. It slid shut behind him. The craft headlamps faded away when it closed. Gabe used a small flashlight from his emergency backpack to find the still-protruding hilt of the cane sword, and then used that as a handhold on his way down.

Before the launch, he'd tried to remove the sword, but it hadn't budged. He was afraid the metal blade had melted and fuzed to the inside of the broken cannon, that it would never come out, that he would never be able to return it to Lupe. But the sword slid out now, so he took it with him.

After one last hop-jump Gabe stood on surface of the moon with a flashlight in one hand and a sword in the other.

He looked up and kept on looking.

The night sky had always seemed finite to him, like the inside of a ball with a few star-holes poked through it—especially the night sky as seen from the middle of a city, with the pale haze of urban light pollution hiding almost everything else. Even on car trips, even when Gabe had been far enough away from city lights to glimpse the sideways streak of our galaxy and see stars so distant that they looked like smoke or a smear of spilled milk, the sky had still looked finite, like a planetarium projector screen.

This looked different.

Gabe stared at the sky. He stared *through* the sky, through the absence of any sky. He looked into everything else. He felt as though he might fall through it, and never stop, and never want to stop.

MOVE QUICKLY, the Envoy wrote across his field of vision. AND PLEASE, BE CAREFUL WITH THAT SWORD OF YOURS.

The Envoy had stretched itself enough to cover Gabe, his backpack, and the little flashlight in his hand, its substance now so thin that it had become completely transparent. Gabe didn't even notice a purple tint to his flashlight beam, though he saw it through the bubble-helmet of Envoy.

He hop-stepped his way across the stones to the base

entrance. It took him three tries to wrench open the door. Then he passed through the small airlock and sealed the second door behind him.

THERE'S AIR IN HERE ALREADY, the Envoy wrote inside itself. I LEFT NOT VERY LONG AGO, BUT I DID TURN OFF THE ENVIRONMENTAL SYSTEMS BEFORE I WENT. MUCH OF THE HEAT HAS DISSIPATED, AND THE OXYGEN MIX ISN'T IDEAL. WE NEED TO GET IT RUNNING AGAIN.

The inside of the pod looked like a passenger plane with all the seats removed and replaced by jumbles of pipes, tubes, dials, and silver foil. Gabe's little flashlight beam bounced back from the foil and scattered in all directions.

What a mess, Gabe thought. He knew there had to be some sort of order to it all, but it wasn't a kind of order that he could see and understand at a glance. It looked like clumsy chaos instead.

THE LIGHT SWITCH IS OVER HERE, the Envoy wrote. It drew an arrow inside its helmet self.

Gabe turned on the lights and looked around. The pod interior seemed even more randomly chaotic with the lights on. He looked down at his feet, encased in the Envoy suit. A fine layer of moon dust covered them both.

Video screens embedded in the wall flickered on. They showed grainy footage of a mountain landscape in spring.

"What's that?" Gabe asked, confused.

A CHANGE OF SCENERY, the Envoy wrote. IT'S SUP-POSED TO BOOST MORALE FOR HOMESICK COSMO-NAUTS. MOVE THROUGH THIS POD AND INTO THE NEXT ONE. WE STILL NEED TO HURRY.

The Envoy guided Gabe to the environmental controls.

HOPEFULLY THE BATTERIES ARE SUFFICIENTLY CHARGED TO START THE SYSTEM AGAIN, it wrote, and probably shouldn't have.

"What happens if they aren't?" Gabe asked.

NEVER MIND, the Envoy wrote. DON'T WORRY ABOUT IT. BOTH THE SOLAR PANELS AND THE ATOMIC BATTERIES WERE STILL WORKING WHEN I LEFT. TURN THIS DIAL HERE.

It drew a little arrow inside its helmet self. Gabe reached for a dial.

NO, THIS ONE, the Envoy wrote. It drew a more forceful arrow, and then a circle around the right dial.

Between them they managed to get the environ-mental systems cranked up again. Gabe shed the Envoy suit and took his first breath of stale, metallic station air.

The Envoy kept a sticky hold on all the dust and dirt it had accumulated outside. It rolled itself and the dust into one lump, and carefully spit the lump into a corner. Then it made a mouth and took a breath of its own.

"Dirt is dangerous here," it explained, "both to your lungs and to the equipment. All the dirt has sharper edges than the stuff at home. No water or air has moved over the particles to smooth them out."

Gabe shivered and rubbed both arms.

"It'll get warmer," the Envoy said. "Follow me. The observatory is down this way."

It led Gabe to a pod filled with ancient-looking computers, most of them open and spilling out their wires and circuit boards. Something like a submarine periscope dangled from the ceiling. Another window-like screen showed more grainy mountain footage. An actual window took up most of one wall. Gabe saw stars through it.

Small, abstract sculptures lined the windowsill. He leaned in for a closer look. He couldn't tell what any of them were—or if they were supposed to be anything other than themselves. "Did you make these?"

"Yes," said the Envoy, sounding embarrassed. "I spent a very long time here. And I was able to extract more ice from the lunar soil than I needed for drinking water, so I used some of it to make mud and clay. Please don't touch. The little statues don't hold together well."

The Envoy began to tinker with the spilled puddles of electronic equipment.

"We can actually scan the asteroids with this stuff?" Gabe asked, skeptical.

The Envoy sighed. "I know it doesn't look tidy, but this was very advanced equipment in 1974. And I've been improving on it in all the years since. Watch."

A floating map of the solar system burst into existence in the center of the room. It didn't look like a projection. It looked as though the Envoy had somehow shrunk the actual system and squeezed it inside itself. Gabe took one careful step closer. He didn't want to disturb anything. He felt as though touching a projected planet might knock the real thing out of orbit like a flicked marble.

"There," the Envoy said, sounding pleased. "That's more interesting to look at. I've cobbled the model together out of data gathered over forty years, since of course we can't see the whole system at once from any single vantage point. This still gives us something to work with. I'll start making new scans and examine the data I had already collected."

"Sounds good," said Gabe, still watching the projected model. "What should I do?"

"You should sleep," the Envoy told him. "Continue

to investigate your fellow ambassadors, especially the Centauri neighbors you've already met. You might even threaten to make public accusations."

"But I don't know who to accuse," Gabe protested.

The Envoy grinned. "They don't know that. They might panic and reveal themselves by panicking."

"Aha," said Gabe. "So you think I should bluff."

"Just an idea," the Envoy said. "You gather information there. I'll gather it here. We can compare notes after you wake up—unless, of course, you discover our enemies, expose them, and drive them out of our system before then. Good luck. There are bunk beds in the next pod on the left."

The Envoy focused its attention on a bulky monitor, where a mess of numerical data glowed lurid green.

Gabe found a bed.

He was tired. He had been up for a while, and he had seen things entirely new to him. He felt both elated and frayed.

The bunk mattress was thin, like the kind of tiny foam camping mats that never actually stay underneath a sleeping bag. But Gabe didn't have as much weight as he usually did, so the thin mattress still felt comfortable.

Before he fell asleep, Gabe thought of a way to frighten his neighbors.

18

"Greetings, Ambassador," said Protocol.

"Greetings, Protocol," said Gabe. He felt less disoriented this time. The transition between waking life and entangled travel became shorter and smoother with each Embassy visit. "I have a request. Please call a local match for me. I challenge *every* adjacent civilization to a game of my choosing."

Protocol paused. That pause had its own gravity. "Are you certain, Ambassador? The Outlast will be among the representative civilizations called to this match."

Gabe straightened his posture and tried to feel as if he had some authority, though he found it very difficult think of himself as tall while talking to a room that had no visible ceiling. Empty space towered above him.

"I'm certain," he said.

"Very well. Where would you like to meet?"

"An open area," said Gabe. "No trees, no hills."

"Very well," said Protocol again. "I have sent the summons. It is traditional to meet in constellation, which means that you will initially stand in relative positions that model your homeworld locations in miniature. You may then move around as your game requires."

"Thanks, Protocol," Gabe said. He wondered what it would look like if *everyone* stood in constellation. They could form a map of the whole galaxy with a great, big, spiraling crowd of kids.

"You are welcome, Ambassador Gabriel Sandro Fuentes. I hope that you will adequately resolve whatever matter prompted you to do this."

"Me too," said Gabe.

The mirror-door slid aside. Gabe walked through the space where it used to be and followed the corridor into the wide expanse of the Chancery. The clouds were different colors this time. Gabe didn't have words for the colors that they were.

Other ambassadors played their games and went about their business. A tournament of several dozen leaf-throwers lined up at the beach, took aim, and tossed their folded planes over the lake. Swimming and hovering ambassadors judged which gliders flew farthest, which ones flew highest, and which ones flew with the greatest style.

Gabe found a ball dropped by one of the flying games. It was dark and almost clear, as though made out of obsidian, though the texture of it felt leathery in his hand. It was also baseball-size. He brought it with him.

One cloud became a pointing arrow and descended toward an open field, otherwise unoccupied. Gabe also heard a low and gong-like sound boom from the same direction, but everyone else seemed to ignore it. They must not have heard it.

He set out for the cloud arrow place. It was a bit of a walk. He took his time, thinking hard.

Ambassador Sapi came bounding toward him on his way downhill.

"Hello, you extremely stupid person," she said. "What are you up to? And wouldn't you rather be climbing trees? I know I would rather be climbing trees. I'd like to assume that you feel the same. And I need to explain to you, slowly and clearly, that you should not ever catch the attention of a genocidal species. You keep doing that. I wish you would stop."

"Can't climb trees," said Gabe. "Not right now. I have a local match to play." He tossed the ball and caught it while he walked.

"Ah," said Sapi. "We just played one of those. We had to hold a shapeshifting duel first, because the Ven and the Gnoles hate each other and they won't talk without dueling first."

"What's a shapeshifting duel?" Gabe asked.

"That's when you face off, hack your own visual translation, and take turns transforming into the scariest shapes you can think of. The first one to scream, laugh, or drop back into their usual sense of shape loses. *Actual* shapeshifters are best at it, of course, but even they can't mess with someone else's perception for long. Protocol gets snippy if they try. Duels are always fun to watch, but I wish the Ven and Gnole delegates didn't have to go through with it every single time we all meet."

"Why do they hate each other?" Gabe wanted to know.

"I don't remember," Sapi told him. She sounded bored, as though she found the whole idea of hatred boring. "Anyway, we all played a guessing game after the duel. And after *that* we got around to helping the Ven get clear of their exploding star. The less fuel a star has, the less gravity it's got to hold itself together, so then it yawns and stretches and grows until it swallows everything else around it." She snatched the ball away from him in mid-toss and made it grow huge like a monstrous beach ball. Then she heaved it up, caught it with both arms, and squished it back down. "The sun burns out after it gobbles up its planets. That's starting to happen now. But it's only just starting. It'll take a couple of Gnole lifetimes to finish, and Gnoles live a long while, so we still have time to send ships and help the Ven relocate. Once we sorted that plan out, the new guy from Treem wanted to know what kind of music other people play, so we switched over to a singing sort of game."

She tossed the ball back to Gabe and sang a tune to herself. Gabe thought it was a tune, at least. The notes fit together according to a whole different sense of math and rhythm than Gabe was used to.

He fiddled with the ball while they walked. "How did you make it change?"

"Twist it this way," she said, miming a demonstration with both hands. "It'll change color, too, if you whack it hard enough."

Gabe tried it a few times, just to get the hang of it, before twisting it back to baseball-size.

"There you go," said Sapi, approving. Then she gave him an alarmed and curious look. "Wait. Hold on. You're from that dinky little spur of a spiral arm on the other side of the center from me."

"How can you tell?" Gabe asked. He hadn't noticed any geographically identifying characteristics about her, or about anyone. He must not have been looking properly.

"It's obvious," she said. "But nobody from your part of the galaxy ever holds a local game. The Outlast dominate most of the arm just beyond yours. If you call for a complete match, then you'll call *them*. You have to interact with them. *Again*."

"That's the idea," said Gabe.

Sapi stopped walking. "That's every kind of stupid that there is! And stupid is infinite. You're still every single kind."

"Thanks," said Gabe.

"What are you trying to do?" Sapi pressed. "Collective suicide? Or are you trying to make a formal complaint? Conquering types don't much care about reprimands. And no alliance of worlds has been able to slow them down, either, so the very best thing to do is avoid them. Maybe you should reconsider this game?"

"Nope," said Gabe. "No time left. Someone's trying to kill me, and it isn't the Outlast—well, I'm pretty sure it isn't the Outlast. But if I can scare them with the Outlast, then I might find out who they are."

Sapi made an untranslatable noise. Then she made it again. Finally she said something that Gabe could understand. "If you think playing a game with Omegan is the least dangerous option available to you, then your circumstances must be very, very bad."

"Things are bad," Gabe agreed.

"Then good luck playing games with your various enemies."

"Thanks." Gabe smiled what felt like a Zorro-ish smile. "That's what this place is for, isn't it? Playing games with everyone?"

Sapi gave him a long look, shook her head, and ran for the trees. She seemed to prefer running to walking.

19

Gabe was the first to arrive at the designated place. One large circle glowed in the grass. He figured that was his place to stand, his spot in the larger constellation. He stood inside it and tossed the ball from hand to hand.

Ripe arrived next. He walked with each foot lifted high, and he placed each step very deliberately before lifting the next. Gabe lobbed an easy throw in his direction. Ripe let the ball land on the ground in front of him. Then he picked it up with one foot, looked it over, and lobbed it back.

Ca'tth climbed cautiously down from the hills and took his own position close to Ripe. His ears fluttered in a flustered, uncomfortable sort of way, but he caught the ball easily and tossed it back.

Gabe let the visual translation do its work. He kept his gaze relaxed and didn't squint at the others. They looked like two kids to him—one with glowing eyes and no hair, and the other with long, oddly bent legs, but still kids. Both watched him closely, expectant, waiting to learn why he had called them together.

He stalled instead of telling them.

"This is the first game I can remember," Gabe said. "My dad and I would sprawl out in the grass and look at the sky while he tossed a baseball into it. I watched the ball go away and come back, over and over. It made a really satisfying smack each time he caught it, like the ball was saying 'I belong right here.' And then Dad would tell me, with his goofy self-importance, that it was a very great magic to throw something and catch it again. He promised to teach me this powerful magic. Then he did. After that we played catch all the time. We'd toss baseballs whenever he was too happy to know what he wanted to say and whenever he was too angry to say anything and just needed to throw things instead. He had a baseball signed by Luis Gómez, another *tapatío* who played for the Twins. It's gone now. He kept it in the basement, in a little glass box, and our basement doesn't exist anymore. Anyway, this game is the first one I remember."

"Remembering," said Ripe. "We make them out of words and out of games and out of strong, important smells. I remember memory games of hidden incense and berry juices first."

"I remember hiding," said Ca'tth. "My home has many, many, many, many hunting things, so everyone learns early how to hide, how to chase, and how to make a game out of it." He looked around, frowning. "We're too exposed out here. Good for chasing. Bad for hiding."

Jir of the Builders and the Yards jogged up to her own place near the other two. Her long hair twitched, restless.

"What's the first game you remember?" Gabe asked while tossing her the ball.

"Wordplay," she said, catching it. "And counting games. Math and language. We made up our own codes so no one else could understand us. That's what we thought at the time, anyway. It felt private, rebellious. But they were already grooming us for the Ambassador Academy, so it was probably the kind of game we were supposed to be playing." She threw the ball back, hard. The impact stung Gabe's hand. "What are we playing now? I hope it's something with teams. More satisfying to see lots of moving parts and players working together."

Gabe eyed his three neighbors. Maybe it was true that they cared more about leaving their shared corner of the galaxy than making piratical claims in Gabe's solar system, but any one of them might still want to steal some ice on their way out—and then make sure no one complained about it by killing the local ambassador. Any one might be an ice pirate. All three of them might be working together, sharing their evacuation plans and excluding Gabe's planet and species from rescue.

His hand still stung from Jir's throw. His pride still stung from Ca'tth's attempts to exclude him from their games and emergency plans. But he tried not to glower and glare. He tried to carry himself with casual confidence. *More like Zorro,* he thought. *Less like Batman.*

Gabe held up the ball. "We aren't all here yet, but let's start anyway. The game is catch. Sort of. Pretend the ball is something else, something new with every throw. Say what else it might be when you throw it." He tossed the ball at Ca'tth. "This is a question hoping to be answered."

Ca'tth fumbled the ball. "What do you mean, we aren't all here yet? Who are we still waiting for?"

"Omegan," Gabe said. He felt like smiling, but he didn't. *Maybe now you'll all feel as scared and vulnerable as I do.* That thought was satisfying, but it also made Gabe uncomfortable. He set his discomfort aside and kept talking. "I guess the Outlast homeworld is farther away, so he'll take longer to get here from his starting point in the constellation. But I did invite him."

Ca'tth dropped the ball again and stared at Gabe.

"Play the game," he said, but Ca'tth didn't move—not even his ears.

"I have a more important question," he hissed. "Why are you doing this? Why, why, why, so many whys, all the whys there are to ask? Why call for a full match? We've already tried to censure the Outlast, to reprimand the Outlast, to build an alliance against the Outlast. None of it has mattered."

You're still only worried about the Outlast, Gabe thought. *It doesn't occur to you to worry about anything else. It doesn't even occur to you that I might be worried about something else. You're not the one trying to kill me.*

Gabe ignored Ca'tth's question and tried to ignore his own creeping discomfort. He no longer felt as if he were doing something right, or righteous. "Play the game," he said, his voice flat and cold.

Ca'tth didn't pick up the ball. Jir walked over and retrieved it. Her hair lashed back and forth, back and forth, agitated and angry.

"This is empty," she said, and twisted the ball to make it bigger. "This is a vast area of empty space in which nothing now lives. This is Outlast territory. This is dead space." She kept her eyes locked on Gabe. "And you've invited those responsible for massive, galactic extinctions *to come play catch with us?*"

Jir's long tail-hair raged behind her head. She sounded incredulous, hurt, and betrayed. She also seemed to think that the Outlast represented the only danger that any of them should be concerned about—Gabe included. *You're not an ice pirate either,* he thought.

She threw the ball. He caught it and twisted it back down to baseball-size.

"Yes," said Gabe. "I invited him to come and play. That's what this place is for." He tried to speak with casual bravado, but to himself he sounded defensive. "Now the ball is, um, a comet." He tossed it to Ripe, because Ripe wasn't glaring at him.

Ripe stood on his hands and used both feet to catch the ball. "This is a sphere," he said. "Its volume would be two thirds of a surrounding cylinder."

"Don't be so literal," Jir told him. "Make something up."

"This is the sharp-smelling seedpod of a sheltering home tree in last bloom," Ripe decided.

I don't understand you, Gabe thought, despairing. *I don't know what you want or what you're afraid of. Maybe you want to assassinate me for reasons I won't ever get. But I don't think so. I don't think so.*

If none of his neighbors were actually ice-pirate assassins, then he had just brought them together and terrified them with Outlast attention for no good reason. He felt sick.

Ripe tossed the ball to Ca'tth, who caught it and held it.

"Omegan's here," Ca'tth whispered. He sounded less worried now that the danger was clearly visible. He looked ready to run. Jir looked ready to fight—but in a hopeless way, as though she knew that the fight wouldn't matter except as a distraction to help the others escape. Ripe didn't really look ready for anything.

Gabe glanced over his shoulder. Omegan of the Outlast stood apart, watching their game. He did not attempt to come closer, to join them, or to stand where he could hear them.

"Don't talk about evacuation," Ca'tth whispered, his voice still calm and placid as though talking about breakfast or the weather. "Don't talk about where we are, or where we're going, or anything about travel capabilities, or weapons capabilities, or any other capabilities. Don't, don't, don't, don't, don't let him spy on us."

"I don't think he's trying to spy on us," said Gabe. "Look at him."

Ca'tth's ears fluttered like moth wings. "The Gabe keeps looking at the Outlast. Stop it." He threw the ball at Gabe's head.

Gabe fumbled, dropped it, and picked it up again.

"Look!" he insisted. "Look how he's standing apart

where we can clearly see him and where he can't hear us. That's not spying! That's the opposite of spying, a refusal to spy. Maybe he's trying to avoid causing any more damage. Maybe he's trying not to learn any more about us."

Jir cautiously considered the Outlast ambassador.

"Maybe you're right," she said. "But it looks to me like Omegan stands *aloof*, not just *apart*. And I'm not impressed either way. Willful ignorance isn't impressive. A passive objection to genocide isn't nearly good enough." She held out both arms to encompass the four of them. "You see how sparsely our part of the spiral is populated. You're new, so you might not understand what this means. You wouldn't understand how many we've lost. You might not be able to even think about numbers that high. But understand this: *I will not speak to the Outlast.* I will not play games with the Outlast." Her voice was steady, but Gabe heard the rage in it. "Look at us. We're all that's left out of hundreds of thousands of worlds. In a whole spiral arm of our galaxy, there's just us and a few scattered nomads passing through."

"Don't talk about the Kaen!" Ca'tth told her in a sharp whisper. "The Kaen doesn't want to be talked about. And she didn't come to join this game. Their ships are in the chase already, running hard, hard, hard, and we mustn't speak any hints about their running path."

Gabe felt prickly tingles on the skin of his arms. If he were something with fur, like a fox or a cat, then all his fur would have bristled.

Kaen is nearby. Kaen is passing through local space. Kaen was the very first person to talk to me here. She and Sapi were the first to ask me questions. And Kaen has kept an eye on me ever since, standing behind Sapi and glaring. Ambassador Sapi might live far away on the other side of the center, along with the musical Treem and the Ven and the Gnoles who always duel with each other. But Kaen is here, right here, hiding in local space and watching me from a tree branch.

"I'm sorry," he said out loud. "I'm sorry that I called this game together. I'm sorry if I put you in any more danger." He held up the ball. "This is an apology. It's for all of you, but I'm going to throw it to *him*. Everybody else scatter when I do."

He turned, held the ball high so Omegan would see it coming—Gabe wouldn't toss anything at an unsuspecting outfielder, even one culpable in galactic genocide—and then threw hard, unsure if the ball would make it so far. It did. Omegan caught it, clearly surprised.

The other three ambassadors scattered in three different directions.

Gabe took a deep breath. He knew what he needed to know. Now it was time to do something about it.

He took two steps. Then he felt wrenchingly dizzy, and woke up.

20

Gabe woke to find the Envoy shaking his shoulder and his mother's voice practically shouting. "Wake up, wake up, wake up!"

"I'm up!" he said. "I'm up. I know who the pirate assassins are, and I'm up."

"Good," said the Envoy. "Because they've found us. They're coming here. Three more repurposed mining ships are en route and will arrive within the hour. It took them far less time to launch new ships at us than I'd hoped, so it might not have been the best idea to bring you to the moon after all. But you know who they are! Excellent. That's a huge relief. You need to get back to the Embassy to expose them. You need to be sleeping. Hurry."

"I was just about to expose them when you woke me up!" said Gabe, annoyed and still groggy but extremely awake. "I haven't learned how to do the deliberate trance thing yet. How can I get back to sleep now?"

The Envoy frowned its puppetish mouth. "You'll just have to trust me," it said, moving closer. "Good luck to you."

It jumped, smothered Gabe's face, and choked him unconscious.

"Greetings again, Ambassador," said Protocol. "Very little time has passed since your most recent visit. Are you well?"

Gabe crouched on the floor, still choking—even though his actual, Envoy-smothered nose and mouth were very far away.

It worked, he thought. *You can let me breathe now. Please let me breathe.*

He finally caught his breath and kept it. Then he climbed up to standing. His reflection looked unsteady in the mirror-door, and his face was flushed.

"I'm fine," he said, insisting on it, trying to make it true.

"I am glad to hear that," said Protocol, still clearly concerned.

"I'm fine," Gabe said again, to the room and himself.

He stood, and he breathed, and he furiously thought.

"How can I send a message to all the other ambassadors?"

he asked. "If I have a public message or a public accusation, how can I talk to *everyone*?"

Protocol told him without sighing or complaining first. "There is a small platform at the very center of the Chancery. You may address all your colleagues from there. This is rarely done, however."

Gabe stood and thought in furious circles. *I can expose them. This is what we planned to do. I can condemn their ice piracy and assassination attempts in front of absolutely everyone. Then Omegan will know where they are. The Outlast will know. So the Kaen will have to leave the system. They'll have to keep running. That might not necessarily stop them from shooting me first, though.*

Gabe decided what to do.

"Protocol, I need to meet with the Kaen ambassador. Somewhere private and hidden. Somewhere in the forest. Please send her that message. Ask if she would meet me there as soon as possible."

She'll come, he thought. *Even though she didn't come to our local game. She might be keeping her distance, but she'll still need to find out how much I know and how much I might reveal to everyone else. She'll talk to me to find that out.*

"Very well," said the room. "I will send the message and guide you to such a meeting place."

"Thank you, Protocol," said Gabe.

"You are welcome, Ambassador."

The mirror-door opened, and Gabe started running.

He raced across the Chancery, avoiding clusters of ambassadors and their games. He ran as though pursued by more silverfish dragon ships with cannons—which he was, somewhere else, somewhere extremely far away. He made for an arrow-shaped pillar of cloud that descended into the forest in front of him.

Omegan stood waiting at the edge of the trees, still holding the ball from their local game.

Gabe stopped and stumbled, unsure what to do. The two faced each other. Omegan made eye contact this time.

He threw the ball at Gabe. It was a bad, clumsy throw. Gabe scooped it up from where it bounced and rolled.

"Why did you call for me to join you?" Omegan asked. "You should not have. Others will always find out what I learn."

"Then I probably shouldn't tell you why," said Gabe. "But I'll tell you this much: I wanted to scare the other ambassadors, so I used you to scare them for me. You're right. I shouldn't have done that. I wish I hadn't."

Omegan nodded. He watched Gabe for an uncomfortable stretch of time. Then he turned to go.

"Thanks for trying not to learn about us," Gabe told

him. "Thank you for trying not to do any more damage. Please don't watch where I'm going now. Please don't follow me."

"You are welcome," said Omegan as he walked away. "And I will not."

Gabe went searching for Protocol's cloud arrow among strangely shaped trees.

He found it in a small clearing set apart from all the arboreal games. He could hear shouts and laughter, but they all sounded distant and faint.

Gabe stretched out on the ground and tossed the ball at the sky. He did that over and over, performing a very great magic while waiting. He wondered if the attack on Zvezda would wake him up before it killed him, or if he would sleep through it. He wondered which way he would rather have it happen.

He didn't have to wait long.

Kaen stopped and stood at the edge of the clearing, well away from him. She maintained a large amount of personal space.

"I'm here," she said, but Gabe had already noticed. He got to his feet and held back, respecting the distance she had already established. He recognized this expanse of personal space from playground fights—even though he was usually pretty good at avoiding playground fights. Kaen stood outside his reach. If he did anything aggressive then she would have time to notice and respond—either by running or by doing something aggressive back at him. She also faced him directly, a hint that flight wouldn't be her first instinct. She didn't cross her arms. She kept both hands free.

"Ambassador," said Gabe, by way of formal greeting.

"Ambassador," Kaen answered.

"You're in our system," said Gabe. He did not say it as a question or an accusation. "You're on board one of those ships in the asteroid belt between Jupiter and Mars."

"Yes," said Kaen.

She didn't try to duck, dodge, or stall him with dithering. Gabe appreciated that.

"You could have asked for the ice," he said.

Kaen shook her head. "If we had asked, and you said no, then we would have died. If we took the ice anyway and you censured us for it, then you would have revealed our position and we would have died. And at first we had no one to ask. This system had no ambassador when we arrived."

"But now it has me," said Gabe. "So you approached me when I first got here."

"I did," said Kaen. "That was when you threatened us."

"Wait, what now?" Gabe shook his head. "I didn't threaten you. I joked around with Sapi while you held back and glared at me. We barely spoke."

"You threatened us," Kaen repeated. "You mentioned that you had already noticed our ships among the asteroids. Immediately after that you sent a signal to the Outlast ambassador."

"What are you talking about? I didn't . . . Oh. You mean the airplane? That was an accident. I didn't mean to hit Omegan in the head with a leaf-paper airplane."

"Did you intend to speak with him every other time you've come here?" Kaen demanded. "Was that also an accident? And did you *accidentally* call for a local match that would include the Outlast, putting all of us in more danger? Why did you do that? Are you trying to suck up to the Outlast? Do you actually think that they'll spare this system out of gratitude? They won't."

Oops, Gabe thought. *She thinks I've been conspiring with Omegan the whole time. No wonder she sent black holes and huge mining bugs after me. It was self-defense. And I'm not at all sure how to untangle this now.*

The two watched each other in wary silence until Gabe broke the tension by laughing.

"What?" Kaen looked more surprised than insulted.

"This is my fault," he said. "Well, no. It's the Outlast's

fault, but I stumbled into it. I'm sorry about that. And now you're stalling, because your mining ships need more time to close in on me and fire their drills. I'm on the far side of moon, by the way, facing away from the planet. Facing you. I'm stranded there. Helpless. No one on Terra will notice if the base explodes, no matter how bright and spectacular the blast." He smiled. He was Zorro facing down a line of muskets.

Kaen stared at him, openly incredulous. "Why are you telling me this?"

Gabe took a step back, extending the distance of their shared comfort zone. He dropped the ball and held both hands out sideways to show her how empty they were.

"I'm telling you because there's no such thing as safe," he said. "There's only trust. I need you to trust me when I say that you have official permission to hide in our system and share our ice."

Kaen kept her voice cautiously neutral and her posture absolutely still. "Why?" she asked again. "We tried to kill you."

"And you're trying again," said Gabe. "Right now. I don't think I can stop you, not even if I did make a public complaint." Lupe would have hated this admission of weakness. Dad would have too. Fighters prefer to go down in glory. Fighters worry about losing strength forever if they once admit it isn't there. But Gabe wasn't a fighter, no matter how tightly he held on to the rage that still simmered at his foundations, no matter how much he wanted to make someone else feel what he felt. This time he wouldn't lash out, wounded. He could be better than that. He was an ambassador.

"If all this is true," Kaen said carefully, "and if these are your very last moments, then you still have time to hurt us by revealing where we are. The Outlast would find us. And even if they didn't, it would still matter for other systems to know that the Kaen took guest gifts without local permission. Ports and docking rights would close to us. You can still hurt us before you die."

"Tempting," said Gabe. "Omegan wasn't far away, last I saw him. I could go right now and tell him where you are."

Kaen shifted her weight, obviously prepared to tackle him if he tried.

"Or I could at least threaten to do that," Gabe pointed out. "I could threaten you and make demands. But no. I won't."

"Why not?" she asked him.

"If I did sic the Outlast on you—which might be harder than everybody thinks, since Omegan is trying really, really hard not to learn *anything* about *anyone*—but if I did manage it, and they came to our system looking for you, they would also find us. That's worth avoiding."

Kaen nodded. "True. Is that why you're offering to help us instead?"

"No," said Gabe. "It's not. I'm doing this because my best friend's house used to be a stop on the Underground Railroad. And because it still is a stop on the Underground Railroad. You're trying to make your way north. You're crossing the desert. You need water. I won't be the one who finds you and turns you in. I won't tell the people with guns where you're hiding. I will not do that."

Gabe's anger stung him like a baseball caught without a glove. It felt painful and satisfying. He didn't try to hide it. He held it in his voice, and he let Kaen hear just exactly how angry he was—but he also held it close. He kept it his own. He threw absolutely none of it at her.

"I'm offering the Kaen emergency hospitality," he said. "Hide in the asteroids. Take some ice. In exchange, I'll need a ride from the moon I'm on back down to the planet I'm from. I'll also need you to stop trying to kill me. Do you accept this offer?"

Gabe waited. He wondered if the mining ships had reached the moon yet, if they had landed on the surface. Maybe they were scuttling toward Zvezda on their many metal legs at that moment, drill cannon glowing, prepared to shoot holes in the walls that kept Gabe alive.

Kaen took two steps closer, closing the distance between them. "I accept your offer of refuge and resources. I'll tell the fleet captains to call off the attack and send you a transport."

"Thank you," said Gabe. "Please hurry."

She nodded once and disappeared.

Gabe wished he knew how to wake up so easily. He wasn't sure which mental muscle to flex. He stood alone in the center of the clearing, in the forest that was not a forest, surrounded by trees that were not trees and that grew according to different rules. He tried to wake up.

When Gabe left the Embassy, finally, he didn't wake up. Instead he dreamed himself into an actual dream, the sort that people usually have: a scrambled mix of hope, fear, memory, and things translated into other things.

He dreamed about his family, all of them together. They didn't look like themselves. The twins kept turning into their pets and back again. Noemi also became a duck sometimes. She said "meow" no matter what she was.

They sat on a blanket, in the grass, in the park. Dad had prepared a picnic. He was still nimble at opening Tupperware, even when he was an eagle instead of himself.

Gabe closed his eyes, smelled the spices, and tried to guess what each dish might be from the smells that followed every open lid. If Gabe had shifted between shapes like the rest of his family, he hadn't noticed. And he was not afraid. He didn't worry that they might be noticed, seen, shot, arrested, deported, assassinated, or invaded. He did not fear conquering Outlast or men with guns and ICE written in white letters over black vests.

Gabe ate his father's cooking, made his mother laugh, chased toddler siblings with Lupe, and none of them were afraid of anything at all. But Gabe didn't remember this dream when he woke up.

The station pod was so unfamiliar that Gabe had no idea where he was, or even who he was, or why he sailed through the air when he jumped out of bed and through lunar gravity. After that he was reasonably sure that he was Gabriel Sandro Fuentes, the ambassador of Terra and all Terran life.

He stumbled into the next pod and found the Envoy. It stood very still, neck craned to peer through a station window. The other window showed grainy video footage of a scenic Russian landscape.

"The ships have arrived," the Envoy whispered. Mom's voice sounded stretched and thin coming through the Envoy's craned neck.

Four mining ships coiled outside and faced the station. Gabe could barely see them in the dark. Each was visible only in the dim glow from the station window and the red glare of their drill cannons.

"I'm sorry, Gabe," the Envoy whispered, tense and quivering. "I shouldn't have brought you here to this defenseless place."

Gabe stood at the window. He held up one open hand, unsure if the gesture would translate at all. Then he waved.

"What are you doing?" the Envoy asked.

"We might be okay," said Gabe. "If she sent the message in time, then we might be okay."

The red glow of the cannon drills did not fade—but the drills didn't fire, either.

Another craft landed behind the four mining ships. The wake of its engines blasted waves of gray dust across the surface of the moon and smacked small stones against the station window. Gabe and the Envoy both flinched. Gabe listened hard for the hiss of escaping air.

The new vehicle looked completely and in every way different from the mining ships. It was green, jade-colored, and it clung to the lunar rock with four sets of landing gear shaped like cat claws.

The Kaen are a mix of different species, Gabe remembered.

Different civilizations, different kinds of ships. That one kind of looks like a flying Mayan artifact, like another Christmas present for Mom to make her homesick. She would hate it. She loathes the idea that aliens visited us thousands of years ago, that they get credit for building our pyramids.

The Envoy spoke with Mom's voice. Gabe was glad to hear the voice. It really was familiar and comforting, now.

"What's happening, Ambassador?"

"I negotiated a truce," Gabe said. "I think it worked. I think that might be our ride home." He took in a long, deep breath. Then he let the breath out and realized that he no longer knew what the word *home* meant, exactly. He didn't know what part of the world to return to.

Mom, Lupe, Noemi, Andrés, and all the pets would be waiting for him at Frankie's house, in Minneapolis, right smack in the middle of North America. He knew that he should join them there. He knew that he needed to help care for the twins and the pets. He knew that he needed to make plans with his fractured family, to figure out where they were going to live now that a black hole had eaten their duplex. He needed to learn how to cope with the constant anxiety that Mom might still disappear at any time. Gabe knew that he should get back to them as soon as he possibly could. But he also knew that his father was on his way south at that moment, in exile.

He had no way to return for at least a decade—unless someone happened to go looking for him, someone with a spaceship, someone who could ride down to any part of the planet that they chose.

The new ship opened its hatch. A small figure with only two legs emerged from the Kaen transport and bounce-walked across the lunar surface.

Gabe and the Envoy both hurried through the station to the entrance airlock.

Gabe spotted his great-grandfather's cane sword there, resting against a wall. He picked it up, felt reassured by holding it, and then set it back down. He didn't want to be holding a weapon in this next moment.

The inner door of the airlock opened. A figure much the same height and shape as Gabe came through it, encased in a dark-green suit. The suit helmet also looked like jade. It looked very much like the saltshaker that Gabe's family used to have in the kitchen, when they used to have a kitchen. It looked like the Olmec had carved this helmet in ancient Mexico.

"No," Gabe said to himself. "No, no, no. That's ridiculous. Mom is going to be so pissed."

He recognized his fellow ambassador as soon as she removed her helmet. She looked exactly like she did in the Embassy—broad nose, high cheekbones, skin a shade or two darker than Gabe's own—but the two of them were not in the Embassy. They faced each other with no translation between them. Gabe squinted, just to be sure.

"You're human," he said. "How can you be human?"

Ambassador Kaen responded in a language that Gabe did not understand.

Acknowledgments

This book has debts. Big ones.

Thanks to Guillermo Alexander, Kay Alexander, Bethany Aronoff, Leonora Dodge, Sara Logan, Sasha Sakurets, Kathryn Sharpe, Joy Nelson, and Tim Hart for their knowledge of immigration law, social services, secret railroads, Russian translations, Mexico, Guadalajara, quantum physics, and cane swords.

Thanks to Melon Wedick, Jon Stockdale, Ivan Bialostosky, Nathan Clough, Haddayr Copley-Woods, Barth Anderson, David Schwartz, Stacy Thieszen, and Karen Meisner for their insights, critiques, and support. Thanks to Mel Logan for the coffee.

Thanks to everyone at McElderry Books and BG Literary, most especially Karen Wojtyla, Annie Nybo, Michael McCartney, Siena Koncsol, Joe Monti, Tricia Ready, and

Barry Goldblatt. My name is the one sprawled across the front cover, but publishing is a collaborative art.

Thanks to Carlos Fuentes, Sandra Cisneros, Gene Roddenberry, and Ursula K. Le Guin for their stories of the borderlands.

Thanks to Alice for uncountable things.

CONTINUE GABE'S ADVENTURE IN *NOMAD.*

GABE'S ADVENTURES
BORDER ON EPIC.

NOMAD
WILLIAM ALEXANDER
THE NATIONAL BOOK AWARD-WINNING AUTHOR OF *GOBLIN SECRETS*

Zvezda Lunar Base: 1974

Nadia Antonovna Kollontai, the ambassador of her world, was not on her world.

She went walking on the moon. Sunlight bounced off the gray stone around her. She felt intense warmth through her bulky orange suit. The reflected glare blotted out all other stars. It turned the sky into absolute darkness. That felt close and comforting rather than infinite, as though Nadia had hidden both herself and the moon underneath a very thick blanket.

She looked forward to throwing that blanket aside.

"Nadia?" Her radio crackled and sputtered. "Zvezda base to Ambassador Nadia . . ."

"Hello, Envoy," she said.

"By my count your oxygen is running low." The Envoy

spoke Russian, and sounded exactly like her uncle Konstantine. It had borrowed Uncle's voice to seem familiar, familial, and comforting. It did sound familiar, but not especially comforting. Uncle Konstantine and Aunt Marina had had many practical virtues between them, but neither one of them had ever learned how to be comforting.

"Probably," she said, as though she didn't care how much air she had left. This wasn't actually true. She had kept careful tabs on her oxygen.

"Please cut short your unnecessary moonwalk and come back inside."

"On my way," she said, but she circled back the long way around to give herself more room to run.

Nadia took huge and sailing lunar leaps, gaining speed. She felt like she could push herself clear of the moon entirely if she only kicked hard enough. She felt like she could fly through space as her own ship.

She took several smaller steps to slow down when the Zvezda base came back into view.

Gray-and-beige modules of the station lay half-buried in lunar dirt. The dirt was supposed to protect the modules from radiation and small meteors, and maybe it did protect the half that was actually covered, but the robotic shovel had broken before finishing the job. Now it looked like a ruin, a relic of some ancient space age rather than the cutting, rusting edge of Soviet engineering.

· Nadia tried not to be cynical about it. The moon base functioned well enough. She lived there. She breathed and ate there. But Nadia was from Moscow, and asking a Muscovite kid to be anything other than cynical about grand Soviet accomplishments was like asking fish to have eyelids. Besides, Aunt and Uncle had designed most of this place (though only Uncle actually got credit for it), so even though Nadia was proud of their astro-engineering, she had also overheard enough dinnertime grumblings about shoddy shortcuts to know that Zvezda barely held itself together with string and spit. And Nadia loved sarcasm. She loved how it could make any word mean both itself and its opposite.

"Nadia?" the Envoy asked, borrowed voice crackling over the radio. She imagined it peering through curved window glass in one of the unburied base modules, craning a long, purple neck to look for her. "Nadia, have you reached the airlock yet?"

"Not yet," she said, her voice pitched to soothe the worried Envoy. "But I can see it from here. Just a few minutes away."

"Stop," the Envoy insisted. "Stop right there. Don't come any closer. Find something to hide behind."

Nadia shuffled to a stop and looked around. She stood on a flat, featureless stretch of rock with nothing at all to hide behind. "What's wrong?"

"The Khelone ship is here. It is landing soon. It is landing *immediately*. I told you this would be a bad time to go for another idle walk."

"Fantastic," she said, and made the word mean both itself and its opposite. "You said it would be here soon as in *days*, not soon as in *minutes*." She was already running, each step a lunar leap.

"Don't pretend that the word *soon* is more precise than it really is," the Envoy told her. "Have you found cover yet?"

"Maybe." She spotted a small crater, a hole in the face of the moon where some small rock had smacked into it, months or centuries or millions of years ago. She skidded while shifting direction, took two more leaps, reached the crater—and sailed right over it. She had to take several small stutter steps to slow down and double back. Then she hopped into the shallow hole.

Nadia stood still, caught her breath, and finally looked up.

She saw the Khelone ship. It was the only visible thing in the sky besides the sun itself.

"Looks like a barnacle," she said.

"Apt comparison," said the Envoy. "Khelone ships are

living things. The pitted outer hull is a grown shell. Are you somewhere safe?"

"I think so," Nadia said. "Mostly. Probably."

The Envoy made a *pbbbbbbt* noise of nervous exasperation. "The force of the Khelone landing will throw a wave of dust and stone in all directions. One of those stones might shatter your helmet, or puncture your suit. That would be almost fitting. We survived a harrowing rocket launch, nearly exploded before we left the atmosphere, and barely managed to land out here. You have lived through impossible dangers already. Now you might be killed within sight of safety, by the very ship you summoned here, because you couldn't resist another unnecessary moonwalk."

"Can't bite your own elbow," Nadia said. It was one of Uncle Konstantine's expressions, and meant essentially the same thing as "so close and yet so far." He always said it with a shrug. Uncle had had lots of expressions, as though he were in some sort of hurry to become a folk-wisdom-dispensing old man—which would never happen now. He had lived long enough to become grumpy, but not long enough to be old.

Nadia turned her thoughts around to walk carefully away from memories of Uncle Konstantine and Aunt Marina.

"I have no elbows, Ambassador," the Envoy said with Uncle's voice.

She tried to crouch down in the crater. It wasn't easy. Cosmonaut suits did not lend themselves to crouching. "Say something nice. I might be about to die, and then your scolding complaint about elbows will be the last thing I'll ever hear. How sad. Say something nicer than that."

"Keep your head down, Nadia," the Envoy said. "Please don't die."

The Khelone ship threw a burst of energy at the ground to slow itself. That kicked up a wave of dust and stone, which expanded outward from the landing site in silence. Nadia tried to keep her head down, but small stones still smacked into her suit and helmet.

She had very carefully appropriated this suit before coming to the moon. It had once belonged to Valentina Tereshkova, the first female cosmonaut—and, prior to Nadia's flight, the only female cosmonaut. At that moment Nadia worried more about damaging the space suit of Valentina Tereshkova than she worried about dying from the damage. She idolized Valentina. The cosmonaut had repaired and reengineered her Vostok space-craft *while already in orbit*. It never would have landed again otherwise. That was an embarrassing state secret, but Nadia came from a family of rocket engineers so she knew about it anyway.

The small, pelting debris settled down. Nadia didn't hear any hissing noises from Valentina Tereshkova's borrowed suit.

"Nadia?" the Envoy asked, worried.

"Still here," she said.

"Excellent," said the Envoy. "Now please hurry back. Try to reach the station before our guest does."

Nadia Antonovna Kollontai was born on April 12, 1961. Yuri Gagarin launched into space on the same day. He was the first human to do so—or at least the first to come home again afterward.

In 1969 Nadia became the ambassador of Terra and all Terran life. She was eight years old at the time. Ambassadors are always young. She lived with her aunt and uncle, and she handled intergalactic incidents on behalf of her planet. She did so in secret. Most human ambassadors do.

Meanwhile her aunt Marina and uncle Konstantine worked on the Zvezda base. Americans had just landed on the moon, so lunar goals had fallen out of favor in the Soviet space program. Uncle Konstantine convinced his project leaders to send a few rockets and drop a few modules of moon base by remote control, but the project ended there. Zvezda sat unfinished, unoccupied, and already abandoned.

Then Ambassador Nadia needed an off-planet site to arrange a meeting and hitch a ride.

She stowed away aboard the last N1 rocket to Zvezda in August 1974. After that she spent more than a month eating cosmonaut food from toothpaste tubes, taking long moonwalks, and waiting for the Khelone ship to arrive.

Up close it still looked like a towering barnacle.

Nadia wondered what it was like to swim through space the way fish swam in water, no barrier between yourself and all the nothing that there ever was. She wondered what it was like to be a living ship. Then she stopped wondering so she could wrestle with the Zvezda airlock latch. It opened on the third try. Nadia climbed through the airlock, sealed both the outer and the inner doors, and then lifted her helmet visor.

The entrance module looked like the body of an airplane without passenger seats. It did not look hospitable or welcoming. It was a mess, an inauspicious place to make first contact. Engineers had no sense of ceremony. The ones in her family didn't, anyway, and she expected other engineers to be pretty much the same.

The Envoy scootched across the metal floor. It raised up its long neck and puppetlike mouth.

"Ambassador," it said, borrowed voice dryly formal.

"Envoy," Nadia answered. "Have you heard anything from our guest?"

"Not yet."

Nadia nodded. Then she started to pace. She could see the Khelone ship outside, through the module's single actual window. The opposite side of the module held a video screen pretending to be a window, one that showed looping footage of a scenic mountain view. Someone back home—definitely not Uncle Konstantine, but someone else on his team—believed that artificial scenery would benefit homesick cosmonauts. Nadia didn't find the fake window beneficial. She tried to ignore it.

"Please stand still," said the Envoy.

"I'm thinking," said Nadia.

"Must you always walk while thinking?" the Envoy asked. "Does your brain even work without the kinetic motion of your feet? You're making me nervous." It tinkered with a lumpy piece of machinery in its nervousness. "I hope the translator works. I did the best I could, but we have only so much equipment to work with here. Visual information may be distorted."

"We'll make do," said Nadia. "But stop fiddling around. You're just going to break it."

She expected the translation device to break anyway. She had expected the rocket that brought them here to explode on the launchpad. She inherited this kind of cheerful hopelessness from Aunt and Uncle—especially from Aunt Marina. "Engineers, rocket scientists, cosmonauts; they all know that things will probably break, fall over, and explode," her aunt would say. "But they're always so happy to be wrong."

Something knocked on the outer hatch of the airlock.

"Poyekhali," Nadia said. "Here we go."

Nadia resealed her helmet and climbed back inside the airlock, closing the inner door behind her.

She had met aliens before. She was an ambassador. Her whole job was to meet and communicate with the representatives of alien civilizations. But none of those meetings had ever happened in person. Nadia had never spoken with one of her colleagues while actually awake. Ambassadors used very strange physics to dream themselves elsewhere. They met in the Embassy, in the very center of the galaxy, without actually having to physically travel—which was good, because it would take many thousands of years to travel so far, even at the speed of light.

Unless you knew how to take shortcuts.

The knock came again. Nadia opened the outer door.

A turtle-shaped suit climbed inside on four legs. It

kicked the door shut with one hind leg, stood up, and considered Nadia through a dark helmet visor. She considered it back. Then she reopened the inner door and gestured inside.

In the Embassy, while dreaming Embassy dreams, Nadia's fellow ambassadors looked human to her. Communication always required more than words. Facial expressions, gestures, postures, behaviors, and games all needed translation, so her colleagues always looked human. Nadia would see them smile, frown, and wave hands in familiar sorts of ways. But she had also learned how to squint and sneak secret glances at the *actual* shapes of the other ambassadors. She could see them as they saw themselves, if she wanted to. And whenever she did that, she always compared their alien appearance to familiar sorts of animals: *That one looks like a flying bear. This one looks like a wolf-fish—or a wolf-mermaid. A fish bitten by a werewolf, maybe.* The other ambassadors never *really* looked like the animals she compared them to; they looked like themselves, and utterly alien to her. Nadia's brain would just try to fit new shapes into old words, because brains like to do that.

The Khelone really did look like turtles, though—or else like tortoises, the kind with long legs and very long necks.

Nadia lifted her helmet visor. The Khelone's helmet folded back inside its suit to reveal large eyes and a turtle-like beak.

"Translation ready?" Nadia whispered.

The Envoy pushed the lumpy translation node toward them. Pale lights flashed and flickered in the center of it.

Nadia's surroundings shifted. She no longer saw the inside of the Zvezda station pod. Instead she saw mountains. Footage from the fake window screen leaked out of its frame to surround her. The view looked grainy, awkward, and false. It gave her a headache.

"Can you turn down the scenery?" she whispered.

The Envoy made adjustments. The grainy mountain landscape flickered and faded away. Then the Khelone changed shape to become human-looking. He wore a brown leather jacket and an aviator's scarf, like a kid dressed up as a biplane pilot. He also looked like a young Yuri Gagarin—the very first cosmonaut.

Nadia did not approve. Everyone she knew in school had had a huge crush on Yuri Gagarin. The whole Soviet Union had had a huge crush on Yuri Gagarin. And Nadia had squeezed her aunt's hand while filing by Yuri Gagarin's coffin at the grand state funeral. It felt wrong in every way to see an illusory version of him now.

She concentrated hard and tried to change how the Khelone looked to her, but it didn't work. Nadia had never been good at manipulating her own translated perceptions. She wasn't any good at fooling herself.

The Envoy scootched off to the side and shifted between several uncomfortable shades of purple. It didn't like being there. Its purpose was to choose and guide ambassadors, not to participate in diplomatic conversations. Nadia was responsible for the actual talking.

"Hello," she said to her invited guest, voice carefully formal and respectful. "I am Nadia Antonovna Kollontai, ambassador of Terra and all Terran life." (The word *Earth* always sounded more official in Latin.)

"Hi," he answered, his voice neither respectful nor formal. He grinned with Yuri's wide grin. "I'm Remscalan of the Khelone Clusters. Call me Rem."

"Welcome," Nadia said, a little wary now.

"Thanks." Rem looked around. Nadia wondered what he saw, exactly. She wondered what the makeshift visual translation looked like to him. He used to be an ambassador himself, when he was still a Khelone kid and not yet an adolescent pilot, so the translator should work well for him—but it was a clumsy sort of translation compared to the Embassy. "I'm amazed you're alive out here," he said. "This is a bare-bones tent you've pitched."

Nadia bristled. She tried not to. Hadn't she just called Zvezda the rusting edge of Soviet technology in the privacy of her own head? But she lived here, and her own family had helped to design this place, throw it through the void, and build it on the moon. She had every right to mock her own home. The Khelone didn't.

"We're only just learning how to leave the planet," she said, her voice barely diplomatic. "It wasn't easy to arrange the neutral meeting place that you needed."

Rem gave her a long look, and then held up both hands. "Khelone ships can't land on planets as large as yours. Well, we *can*, but we'd never be able to take off again afterward. Escape velocity is difficult for those of us who've never had to bother with planets at all. And getting stuck planetside wouldn't be useful. You did call me here for transportation, right? You gave our new ambassador rare maps in exchange for a ride."

Nadia had pieced together maps and information from the Seventh Fiefdom, the Volen Enclaves, and the People of the Domes. Those maps were all rare because the Outlast had since swallowed the Seventh Fiefdom, the Volen Enclaves, and the People of the Domes. Those three civilizations were now extinct.

"I've heard you can travel fast," she said. "That you're good at taking *shortcuts*."

Rem rested both hands behind his head. "True. I made it here almost instantly."

I sent you a message more than a year ago, Nadia thought, but didn't say. Time flows differently when you move fast.

"Excellent," she said aloud. "Then I need you to accomplish a momentous and probably impossible feat of piloting skill."

"I'm interested," Rem said, and smiled wider.

The silly leather jacket and aviator scarf is a good translation, Nadia thought. *He really is that sort of pilot. He's delighted to try some new and dangerous thing.*

"We are going to fly into the Machinae lanes," she said.

Rem gave her a sideways look. "I think your translation node just broke. I definitely heard the wrong preposition."

"We're going inside the lanes," Nadia said again.

He shook his head. "Are you joking? I can't tell if you're joking. No one goes into the lanes, silly human. We skip across the surface instead. We can sidestep light speed by riding in the Machinae's wake, skimming right across those rippling waves of warped space-time. *Barnacle* and I are better at that kind of wake-hopping than anyone—"

Nadia tried not to laugh. The ship's name probably sounded more dignified than *Barnacle* in Rem's own language.

"—We can fly close to the lanes and their scrambled sense of gravity more skillfully than anyone else you could possibly find. But no one ever flies *into* the lanes."

"Untrue," Nadia said. "Witnesses tell me otherwise. The astronomers of the Seventh Fiefdom saw ships emerge from inside the lanes. So did the People of the Domes. Cartographers of the Volen Enclaves heard it happen while making their song-maps."

Rem looked serious now. His posture lost its casual, adolescent unconcern. "I hear bad things about the Fiefdom, Domes, and Enclaves. What happened to them *after* they saw ships fly from the lanes?"

"They all died," Nadia told him.

In her memory she heard heavy boots outside a cupboard door, though she tried very hard not to.

"You used to represent the Khelone," she went on. "Honor the trade I negotiated with the ambassador who took your place."

And you're curious, she added, just to herself. *Now that you're starting to think this is possible, you really want to try it. I can tell. Even through the fuzzy translation, I can still tell.*

Rem tossed the end of his aviator scarf over one shoulder in a cartoonishly rakish way.

"Fine," he said. "Come aboard."

Masks that transform the wearer.
A flute that separates a girl and her shadow.

What fateful magic lies hidden in the heart of Zombay?

Don't miss *Goblin Secrets*, a National Book Award Winner,
and its companion, *Ghoulish Song*, by William Alexander.

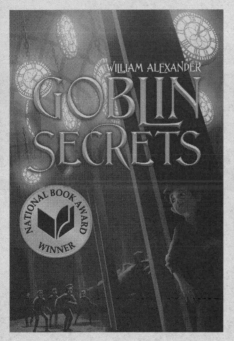

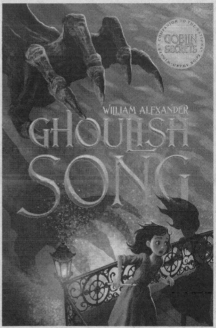

★"Gripping and tantalizing."—*Kirkus Reviews*, starred review

"It was hard to stop reading *Goblin Secrets*, and I didn't want the book to end!
The author's imagination is both huge and original. More, please, Will Alexander!"
—Ursula K. Le Guin, author of the Earthsea Cycle

"Funny, smart, and gorgeously written. When I grow up, I want to be Will."
—Jane Yolen, author of *The Devil's Arithmetic*

PRINT AND EBOOK EDITIONS AVAILABLE
From Margaret K. McElderry Books | KIDS.SimonandSchuster.com

BRAVERY ISN'T MEASURED BY SIZE. IT'S MEASURED BY HEART.

HOW BRAVE IS YOUR HEART?
Visit Mouseheart.com to see.